Percy H. Fitzgerald

A Famous Forgery

being the story of the unfortunate Doctor Dodd

Percy H. Fitzgerald

A Famous Forgery
being the story of the unfortunate Doctor Dodd

ISBN/EAN: 9783337268237

Printed in Europe, USA, Canada, Australia, Japan

Cover: Foto ©Andreas Hilbeck / pixelio.de

More available books at **www.hansebooks.com**

A FAMOUS FORGERY

BEING

THE STORY OF "THE UNFORTUNATE"
DOCTOR DODD.

BY

PERCY FITZGERALD, M.A., F.S.A.,

AUTHOR OF "NEVER FORGOTTEN," "THE LIFE OF STERNE,"
"BELLA DONNA," &c.

LONDON:
CHAPMAN AND HALL, 193, PICCADILLY.

1865.

LONDON
PRINTED BY C. WHITING, BEAUFORT HOUSE, STRAND.

TO THE

RIGHT HONOURABLE

LORD ARUNDELL OF WARDOUR.

PREFACE.

———◆———

THE following " Story " is not put forward as a
biography of Doctor Dodd—who, for many good
reasons, would be wholly unworthy of regular bio-
graphical treatment—but as a picture of a certain phase of life and manners towards the end
of the last century. The reader will have before
him a character very familiar to those days—a leading actor in the wild society of the time—the well-
known figure of what was called the Macaroni
Clergyman. The semi-barbarism of judicial procedure, and the horrible, but dramatic, incidents which
then attended the final process of the law, all deserve
study and illustration, and could in no way be so
conveniently illustrated as by the singular and
almost romantic history of " the unfortunate Doctor
Dodd." It may be added, also, that the subject was
long ago pointed to, in a Quarterly Review of high
authority, as worthy of being seriously taken up; and

that Doctor Doran, in one of his " Pictures," has
drawn a very faithful portrait of this unlucky divine.

Not to crowd the page with foot-notes and references, I may mention that nearly everything that is
known about Dodd will be found in the following authorities: in Boswell; Wraxall; the Life of Romaine ;
Life of Horne; Toplady's Memoirs; Archenholtz's
Travels ; Selwyn's Memoirs ; Angelo's Memoirs ;
Walpole's Diary and Letters; Thicknesse's Memoirs;
Hawkins's Johnson ; the contemporary Newspapers ;
the Town and Country Magazine, 1773 (the magazine which, found in the window of an old inn, so
delighted Charles Lamb with its *Tête-à-têtes*) ; the
Magazines and Newspapers of 1777; Villette's Account; the published Trial ; Taylor's Recollections;
Croft's Love and Madness; together with many passages and allusions up and down, through such reading as Garrick's Letters and Nichol's valuable Anecdotes.

This little Memoir has also profited by the kindness
of my friend Mr. John Forster, who has allowed me
to use his most curious collection of newspaper " cut-
tings," pamphlets, and engravings; all relating to this
" unfortunate divine." It seems to have been made
by some contemporary admirer, and includes almost
every scrap of published town gossip that could bear
on the subject.

P. F.

January, 1865.

CONTENTS.

CHAPTER THE FIFTH.

CHAPTER THE SIXTH.

CHAPTER THE SEVENTH.

CHAPTER THE EIGHTH.

CHAPTER THE NINTH.

CHAPTER THE TENTH.

CHAPTER THE ELEVENTH.

CHAPTER THE TWELFTH.

CHAPTER THE THIRTEENTH.

CHAPTER THE FOURTEENTH.

A FAMOUS FORGERY.

BOOK THE FIRST.—WEST HAM.

CHAPTER THE FIRST.

INTRODUCTION.

THE story of this unhappy clergyman has not been told before; yet its dim, indistinct outline is, in a sort of general way, familiar to many persons. This acquaintance seems to resolve itself into three main features—that of the centre figure being a clergyman, that his offence was a forgery, and that, through the terribly severe laws of his country, he suffered death for the crime. The "Execution of Doctor Dodd" is, perhaps, the idea most distinctly present to all, when they think of his name. The flurry of the days between his sentence and death has in it something almost lurid; and idolators of Boswell's book—and there are such—will own to there being a sort of horrid fascination in the passages he devotes to this incident.

B

The story is worthy of being told, because no English social event of that character, before or since, ever excited so much absorbing interest. We may gather some faint notion of the sensation spread over the whole kingdom, if we were to read one morning of the arrest, say, of some graceful writer and popular preacher, and of his committal to a London gaol, charged with some barbarous crime, which was to bring with it the penalty of death. Yet, in those days, human life was judicially cheap, and London eyes were used to the spectacle of processions to the gallows. The extreme penalty of the law, as it is called, viewed from the present century, we are apt to accept as a measure of guilt, which, in those days of bloody dispensation, it was not.

The wretched clergyman was the victim of the old, stupid, mulish British complacency, which has so often fancied itself doing something Spartan and splendid, when it is only cruel and ridiculous; which, as Lord Macaulay has shown, must have its recurring fits of morality, and calls for a victim now and again, to waken up its slumbering complacency: which once shot an admiral "to encourage the rest," and hanged Doctor Dodd to show the surrounding world a spectacle of stern, unflinching morality.

For the offence which Doctor Dodd committed, such a punishment was unsuited—and almost unmerited. Even weighing the moral delinquency nicely, there was no such tremendous guilt involved in the offence. The details now about to be presented have never been collected before, and may be said to be new to a nineteenth-century reader.

CHAPTER THE SECOND.

AT COLLEGE.

Down at Bourne, in Lincolnshire, a certain Reverend William Dodd was vicar, early in the reign of George the First. The little town was on the very edge of the Fens, and young William Dodd had before his eyes the quaint old Hôtel de Ville of the place, which was of some beauty, and of great antiquity. A thoughtful, studious man, with "a dear, pale face," his son described him long after.

This son — the eldest — the notorious William Dodd, LL.D., was born there, on the 29th May, 1729. There was also a second son, who afterwards grew up to be the Reverend Richard Dodd, a working clergyman, but about whose story—there being no painful notoriety to make him stand out—history is almost silent.

Over this child, at its studies, the "dear, pale face" was bent very often, and succeeded in implanting a curious fancy for study and general reading. Young William Dodd took ardently to books; and, when only sixteen years old, was fit to be entered at Cam-

bridge. He was matriculated a sizar of Clare Hall
on March 22, 1746, and was placed under Mr. J.
Constant, afterwards Archdeacon of Lewes. Men
holding these offices at universities must have a
singular advantage over other men, in being thus
familiar with the early years of those, who may turn
out famous for good or evil; and a veteran college
director might find some entertainment in checking
off his earlier judgments by a later experience. But
mere official routine, in most instances, must deaden
this spirit of observation.

Laurence Sterne had quitted Cambridge but a few
years before. It will be seen later how like, in some
points, were the two clergymen. The only person of
mark we can trace as being at Clare Hall with Dodd,
is Parkhurst, who afterwards became familiar to
scholars from the well-known "Lexicon." Here,
however, he found a friend, to whom he seems to
have been attached, with all the ardour of college
affection, but who died early, before completing his
studies. His image came back upon Doctor Dodd—
then under very altered circumstances—full thirty
years later:

> Nor less, for thee, my friend, my Lancaster,
> Blest youth, in early hours from this life's woes,
> In richest mercy borne.

But of this promising youth nothing more of interest
is known.

During his college career Dodd was remarkable for
diligence, and for some success in his studies. He
"attracted the notice of his superiors," we are told,
by his special attention to his books. He could, how-

ever, find time for literary labour; and, at the age of eighteen, sent forth the first of the long train of books which he was hereafter to launch so steadily upon the town. This was a quarto pamphlet, entitled "A Pastoral on the Distemper among the Horned Cattle, or Diggon Davy's Lament on the Loss of his last Cow." Considering that this plague was a national calamity, sweeping the whole of Europe, and that Mr. Sterne, down at Sutton, and other divines, were dealing with the subject in their pulpits, such levity would seem to have been in bad taste; but a careless college lad of eighteen might be excused for not weighing the decencies very nicely.

Two years after, the African Princes came to England, and he seized on the opportunity to issue a quarto tract of mild heroics, in the shape of an address from the African "to Zara"—inscribed according to the usual precedent to a person of influence, Lord Halifax—which was later followed up by an answer from "Zara" to the African Prince. These youthful efforts are of the very poorest quality, and suffer sadly by comparison even with the low standard of average "Juvenilia." As such they might claim the usual indulgence, had not their author, later, when more advanced in life, collected them carefully, and presented them to the public in a volume. The same year, 1749, he took his degree, with distinction, and his name is to be found fifteenth on the "First Tripos List," which corresponds to the more modern wranglers and senior optimes.

With this promising beginning he might have hoped to fare profitably in the University. His brother, the Reverend Richard, had gone to Lincoln College, Oxford, and in due time had chosen to become a working curate at Camberwell; *he* was to end decently and with honour, as a fairly endowed rector. But young William Dodd was of different material, and at every step reminds us marvellously of that other clergyman, the Reverend Mr. Sterne, down at Sutton.

It was not likely that the straitened Vicar of Bourne could afford to fetch home his son during the vacation. Young Dodd, therefore, had to spend that season at the University, when it was a dismal and dispiriting solitude, during which time his only comfort seems to have been a blank verse protest, of indifferent merit as a composition, but valuable as a graphic picture of Cambridge manners. He helps us to see the deserted courts, with their smoke-stained windows, which, in term time, were peopled with crowds of heads covered with caps of coloured velvet, calling loudly for the barbers, who were flying across the quadrangles. We see the "lean fellows," and the "jolly jips," the old bed-makers, and the refectory tables covered with black cloth. Young Dodd would seem to have been the only one of his college left to take "commons" in the hall, and had to rise to do homage to a fellow, just as solitary in *his* rank as the youth himself. The trencher off which he had to dine, was a square piece of board "never scraped and sometimes washed." An odd privilege was allowed to the twelve wranglers of the year, who were allowed to choose a squire, and go round the town, asking a kiss from each young girl. Mr. Dodd, who took his

degree in 1749—and took it with distinction, for he was
in the list of wranglers—just happened to be among
the last few who were permitted these rights; for in the
following year, the "ancient custom" was abolished.
"The good-natured ladies," he says, "never were
averse to so laudable a custom. . . . . Scarce
a dry eye was seen on the day when the wranglers
were lost; the peeping maidens observed now and
then one with downcast looks steal along the streets
and muffle his inglorious face in dismal black. The
year 1750 will be remembered with grief by every
Cambridge virgin and future wrangler." This is
merely what in these days would be called the viva-
city of an "ingenious young gentleman," but some-
way in every phase of life, from Cambridge to Newgate, some levity of the gay, frivolous Dodd is always
present. Even at this day there was a "Lucy," of
whom the youth in his loneliness thought tenderly.

He was a very gay youth, fond of Cambridge
pleasures and parties, dressed expensively, and was
noted among his friends as "an ardent votary of the
god of dancing." These pastimes did not interfere
with more important matters; and, in truth, it stands
a good deal to his credit that he should be able to
combine such hostile interests so successfully. Later,
however, the balance became disturbed, and in the
year of his degree he left the University very suddenly, and came up to London.

CHAPTER THE THIRD.

ORDINATION AND MARRIAGE.

YOUNG Mr. William Dodd, now upon Town, brought with him, say his biographers, in their peculiar euphuism, " a pleasing form, a genteel address, and a lively imagination," gifts which, in the year 1749 or 1750, were much esteemed in the great city. He lost no time in putting them to all available profit; and his books having already attracted a little notice, he rushed into every society, and flung himself upon every amusement "with a dangerous avidity." No doubt the excuse that brought him up, was the invariable excuse that brought up from all corners of the kingdom any young literary adventurer who had a play, a history, or a poem in his desk; it being considered necessary to come in person to fight for literary fortune, as Whittington and others had come up for mercantile honours. In his spare moments, he contrived to write and publish some compositions. Among these was another satire, " A Day in College at Vacation ;" a synopsis in Latin of Grotius, Locke, and Clarke, a large portion of which is said to have been the work of Sir John Gilbert; a sort of useful class-book, which must have entailed some serious drudgery; and a more ambitious effort—a burlesque addition to the "Dunciad," with Warburton introduced. He was, no doubt, one of the tribe of "vile scribblers" alluded to by Warburton, in his letters to Sterne; but was wise enough, when grown older, not to provoke the controversial bishop by reprinting it in his collection. These works show a certain industry, and might incline us to suppose that the "dangerous avidity" for London pleasures was a little overstated. He was now but twenty years old.

There was living at this time in Frith-street, Soho, a young person named Mary Perkins, with whom young Mr. Dodd became acquainted. She is said to have been "largely endowed with personal attractions," but, on the other hand, was fatally "deficient in those of birth and fortune." The plebeian name is, indeed, significant; her father was a servant to Sir John Dolben, one of the prebendaries in Durham Cathedral, and had been promoted to be verger. This young person Mr. William Dodd, with his fair prospects in the world before him, had the infatuation to marry on April 15, 1751.

In other respects she seems to have been a very suitable wife; and at the season of her husband's terrible probation, exhibited all the virtues and moral gifts which happily belong to no special rank or station. Nay, though marrying him without bringing a dowry with her, a lucky chance was to help her to one later. She was all through useful, affectionate, and tolerant of his frailties to a remarkable degree;

and if we can trust the dismal apostrophe which issued from his prison cell, he never appears to have repented marrying the verger's daughter :

> Nor thou, Maria, with me! O, my wife!
> Thy husband lov'd with such a steady flame
> From youth's first hour.

And it is certainly to his credit that, even in the days when he was most sought and courted, and when he was most busy with "Miss I——t" and the "two agreeable sisters," he is not ashamed to boast of his nuptial happiness, or to find her a place beside the elegant ladies he was celebrating in gallant rhymes. At Margate he could be in raptures with her. "When by my Charmer's side, my bride, my love, List'ning I drink the music of her tongue. . . . Give me eyes to trace her every amiable perfection," &c.

Her sister, Eleanor, was married to "an upholder," called Porter, in Long-acre. It was a miserable alliance in one sense; and it was recollected nearly thirty years later that the bride and bridegroom appeared in gay colours at the ceremony, though all the town was mourning the Prince of Wales in deepest black. Perhaps Doctor Dodd was resenting the indifferent patronage his elegy had just received.

On this imprudent step, he at once took a house in Wardour-street—not yet lined with *Bric-a-brac* and curiosity shops — and fitted it up at great expense. The news of these proceedings soon drifted down to Bourne, to his father, who presently hurried up to London in sad distress. Friends gathered round; the pressure of remonstrance and entreaty was put upon the improvident youth; and with much diffi-

culty he was brought back again into the straight
and profitable ecclesiastical roadway he had strayed
from. After watching an opportunity to write "An
Elegy on the Death of Frederick Prince of Wales,"
he came back again to Cambridge.

For this performance—which he thought of when
lying in Newgate, bitterly complaining of its having
been overlooked by royalty—he received five guineas
from Mr. Watts. He had also written a comedy,
for which he was to receive a hundred pounds—which
had actually got to a manager's hands, but which he
was obliged to withdraw on pressure from authority.
This comedy shall turn up again later under very
curious circumstances.

On the 19th of October, 1753, he was ordained a
deacon, at Caius College, by the Bishop of Ely—a
prelate to whom he had dedicated his Latin synopsis
of Clarke and Grotius.

Even at this date he had been eagerly looking for
preferment; and this "Elegy" was but one of those
little devices to secure promotion for which he was
later to become notorious. His importunity was almost wearisome; and nearly thirty years after, in a
situation where idle college verses would seem about
the last thing he would think of, he refers to these
academic platitudes with a sort of wounded air, as
though he had been ungratefully repaid for his
panegyric.*

The Wardour-street house was now given up, and
he openly forswore the world and its vanities, with a

* Prison Thoughts, Week the Fourth, where he has a note, "See my
Elegy on the Death of Frederick Prince of Wales. Poems, p. 63."

suspicious ostentation. Not content with mere quiet abnegation, he must proclaim his reformation noisily—through a trumpet, as it were, and from a platform. The platform was a selection of the best passages in Shakspeare, and the trumpet was a preface. "For my own part," he wrote, "better and more important things henceforth demand my attention, and I here, with no small pleasure, take my leave of Shakspeare and the critics. As the work was begun and finished before I entered upon the sacred functions in which I am now happily engaged," &c. With this apology the first symptoms of distrust begin to enter the mind—for who can accept these excuses for so harmless a task as a selection of passages from a writer like Shakspeare? The whole has the air of affectation, if not of cant; and already we begin to see the faint lines and colours of the Macaroni Parson.

But the idea was a very happy one—far better than the well-meaning scheme of the more recent Mr. Bowdler. The selection was directed by much good taste, and even ingenuity. It has been one of the most successful bits of bookseller's task-work; and a stream of editions, of every size and price, attest the popularity of "Dodd's Beauties of Shakspeare." But very few, when they buy the book in shop or stall, think that it is by *the* Doctor Dodd, or of the dismal end of the compiler. Work of this sort, simple as it may seem, disguises a vast amount of secret labour and happy instinct; as, indeed, Goldsmith has shown in a single sentence: "Judgment is to be paid for in such selections, and a man may be twenty years of his life cultivating his judgment."

Curious to say, there was originally prefixed a sarcastic dedication to Lord Chesterfield, which he afterwards cancelled. He could not have divined that this nobleman would have hereafter selected him for his son's tutor. Being now ordained, he forswore pleasure and the belles lettres "finally"—that is, for nearly a year—and entered on his first ecclesiastical service as curate to the Rev. Mr. Wyatt, at West Ham—a clerical pasture, perhaps, dangerously near to London.

CHAPTER THE FOURTH.

WEST HAM.

HERE he spent the most delightful hours of his life. His behaviour—say the newspaper paragraphs, in the detestable "valet" jargon in which they describe every step in his life—was "proper, decent, and exemplary." He took up his new duties with zeal. He is said to have worked laboriously amongst his parishioners, and not to have spared himself in the round of parochial drudgery. Yet he relished these duties, and long after, in his day of trial, looked back to this Ham life very wistfully :

> Return blest hours, ye peaceful days return!
> When through each office of celestial love,
> Ennobling piety my glad feet led
> Continual, and my head each night to rest
> Lull'd on the downy pillow of content!
> Dear were thy shades, O, Ham! and dear the hours
> In manly musing 'midst thy forests pass'd,
> And antique woods of sober solitude,
> O, Epping, witness to my lonely walks.

It was thought at this time that he " entertained favourable sentiments of the doctrines of Mr. Hut-

chinson," and was even suspected of a leaning to
Methodism. But he soon cast off this weakness, and
some seven or eight years later put his thoughts into the
shape of "A Dialogue between a Mystic, a Hutchin-
sonian, and a Methodist;" in which he showed off the
professors of these creeds to considerable disadvantage.
Notwithstanding this backsliding in the direction of
Mr. Hutchinson, his parishioners esteemed him highly,
and chose him as their lecturer on the demise of the
former occupant of that office. Two years afterwards,
a lectureship at St. Olave's, Hart-street, became vacant,
and Mr. Dodd was chosen for this duty also. Then
he suddenly relapsed into literature, not only forgot
his vow of abstinence, but burst upon the town with
a strange novel, which, coming from a working curate,
seems a singular and unbecoming composition.

It was entitled "The Sisters;" which, under the
specious veil of "a warning to youth of both sexes,"
contrives to deal with some free pictures of London
life, the treatment of which suggests the coarse, but
not the vigorous, handling of Fielding and Smollett.
How the laborious curate of West Ham could issue
such a production and not forfeit the favour of his
faithful parishioners and the patrons of the lectureship of St. Olave's, is a riddle only to be solved by the
free temper of the age. The ecclesiastical barometer
was never registered so low. The laity were easy,
and expected no restraint from their priests. There
were many parsons like Trulliber, and many like the
ordinary who attended on Mr. Wild, and whose
pocket was picked of "a bottle screw." The world
was not to be scandalised by "The Sisters," or a

novel of that sort; and six years later the Bishop of
Gloucester was so delighted with the two first volumes
of "Tristram Shandy," that he took their reverend
author round the fashionable world, and made all
the bishops call upon him.

"The Sisters" contain many pictures drawn from
young Mr. Dodd's wild London life. The story is
that of two young girls sent up to London, and
ruined there. There is a hint of Pamela, with sug-
gestions from some of Hogarth's pictorial stories.
The names of the characters are the names of real
persons read backwards. Dookalb, the villain of
the piece, was a Mr. Blackwood, a gentleman who
was said to have injured him, and upon whom he
took this fashion of retaliating. Beau Leicart was a
certain fashionable Mr. Tracey, known as Handsome
Tracey, who had met a pretty girl in the Park—a
butter-woman's daughter—and, seized with an ungo-
vernable passion, had made himself the talk of the town
by marrying her.* Lucy Repook, another of the characters, was put for Lucy Cooper, a notorious lady
who divided the favour of the town with " Kitty
Fisher." She was the lady who furnished the story
which contains a satire finer than ever professional
satirist could furnish.† Lord Sandwich was also introduced, which would seem to support the story

---

* The story is given in detail by Walpole, ii. 126. There is more
about him in Taylor's Recollections.

† To a young nobleman professing " eternal attachment," she hinted
a settlement—as she was sure, she said, he could not bear to see her
miserable and in want, in her old age. " No, by G—," said the young
nobleman, promptly, " for then I could not bear to see you at all."
She used to tell this story herself.

Walpole later circulated as to Mrs. Dodd's relation to that nobleman. Speaking of one of the ladies of the story who was in the habit of taking bank-notes *en sandwich* for breakfast, to show her admirers how little she cared for money, the Reverend Mr. Dodd puts a note to the effect that he had known " at least four, who have excelled and gloried in the same notable feat." There are allusions, too, "to the inimitable Garrick" who "thunders through the crowded theatre," which show that he was familiar with dramatic effects. Most curious, however, is his treatment of his arch villain, Dookalb, or Blackwood, whom he eventually *led to the gallows* and made him suffer " in the most abject and pusillanimous manner ;" and attached to one of his characters was " a large bunch of keys, not unlike those which grace the venerable turnkey of Newgate." He never dreamt, when he gave this flippant description, that he himself was to have a dreadful familiarity with the venerable turnkey of Newgate. Indeed, it is very strange to think how, all through Mr. Dodd's life, little shadows of such an awful final end were cast across his path. It will be seen how, in many directions, he was led to it by a sort of mysterious attraction, and dwelt upon it as upon a favourite subject.

He was about this year — 1752 — appointed to preach " Lady Moyer's Lecture" at St. Paul's, for which he took up the doctrine of the Trinity as his subject. He also plunged into classical learning, issued proposals for a translation of Callimachus, and wrote a play on the Greek model, with choruses, entitled " The Syracusan," which was actually sent

c

to a manager. In these times, parsons were very
busy writing plays, and seeing them acted; nay, and
acting them themselves.*   Strange to say, "The
Sisters" did him no damage; for the following year
the translation of Callimachus came out with a
learned preface, in which Doctor Horne, the Bishop of
Norwich, lent him his assistance. The Reverend Mr.
Dodd was, perhaps, looking for a mitre himself, and
might naturally hope to reach one by his "Callimachus," as later postulants were to do by a play of
Sophocles' or Euripides'. This book had a splendid
list of names "prancing before it." As a more direct
means of promotion, he dedicated it to the reigning
Duke of Newcastle, the desperate adherent of office,
who in his time had made many bishops, and found
them all ungrateful. Meanwhile he was writing sermons, and some years later published *four volumes
quarto* of discourses, a monument of parochial industry.

All this while he was still at Ham:

> Dear favourite shades, by peace
> And pure religion sanctified, I hear
> The tuneful bells their hallowed message sound,
> To Christian hearts symphonious.

He was lecturing at St. Olave's. He could not be
idle, and had his time too well employed to go astray.
These were the more innocent seasons of his life.
No wonder, when the Newgate bells were clanging

---

* It was actually written over to Garrick from Dublin—and this as
no astounding piece of news—that they had a parson there who was
coming out at the theatre, in the character of *Scrub*.

over his head, that the chimes of West Ham should seem very sweet indeed.

The complexion of this "Ham" life seems to have been more a dreamy and pastoral sensuousness than the pious seclusion which he fancied it to be—at least, it is hard to shut out some such impression of what his real temper was, when in the midst of this happy retirement he could strangely break out into a town story too warm in tone to be consistent with an innocent and wholesome state of mind. Side by side with these glowing recollections of "fast" life, on which he evidently dwelt with satisfaction, he could find room for such Della Cruscan fancies as the following :

> With lov'd MARIA by his side,
> As happy as a king,
> See! cheerful William smiling ride
> To taste the balmy spring.
> Beside Earl TILNEY's park they rode,
> Earl TILNEY's grand and gay!

A long flourish follows about "Cheerful William" helping an old man and an old woman with their dog over the palings of "Earl TILNEY's" park, and in happy rapture with himself, exclaiming,

> How much one good well natured deed
> Exhilarates the mind.

The sentimentalism that could expand itself in a hundred and fifty lines of such doggerel, gravely exalt itself from such an act of charity, and almost in the same breath revel in glowing descriptions of London bagnios, is of an unhealthy sort. And it will be found that this was in some sort the pattern of his

life all through—piety and dissipation, religious trea-
tises and the lightest rhymes, the chapel and "the
rooms," public charities and drawing-room gallantry,
all jumbled together.   It was scarcely surprising
that men later came to talk of him as a hypocrite, or
" a whitened sepulchre."   Which, indeed, it does not
appear that he ever consciously was.   It was a well-
meaning sentimentalism coupled with a weakness of
resolution, which made him the prey of any sugges-
tion that presented itself.

CHAPTER THE FIFTH.

"THE MAGDALEN."

ABOUT this time a certain charitable Mr. Bingley began to take up seriously the condition of the female outcasts of society, and set himself to try whether something could not be done for such of this class who were inclined to amend and reform. It was proposed to found an asylum on the principle of those at Rome, and other foreign cities. The state of London manners at this particular season rendered the establishment of such an asylum peculiarly suitable.

Mr. Bingley and his friends got together some three thousand pounds for their purpose. The scheme was warmly seconded; and by none so much as by the young curate of West Ham. The first building was in Prescott-street, Goodman's-fields; and on Thursday, the 10th of August, 1758, it was opened. Fifty petitions were presented, but only ten candidates could be received, and the Reverend Mr. Dodd, who had taken such an interest in the charity all through, was chosen to preach the inaugurative sermon before the governors in Charlotte-street Chapel, Blooms-bury.

The policy of such an institution was loudly condemned at the time; and pamphlets were published
violently decrying the new asylum.   But it prospered
marvellously, and became the most fashionable of
London charities.   When Mr. Sterne, the fashionable clergyman, was preaching for the Foundling
Hospital, his exertions brought in only one hundred
and sixty pounds, while appeals for the Magdalen, by
divines of indifferent gifts, resulted in collections of
thirteen and fourteen hundred.

No doubt there was truth in what was openly said
at the time, that it was a sort of theatrical charity, to
which people hurried for a Sunday's sensation, just
as they had done a few years before to the rantings
of Orator Henley.   The chapel, indeed, offered a sort
of spectacle; and there were melodramatic devices
adopted, which it may be suspected were the devising of
the young chaplain of the institution.   The penitents
were all dressed in uniform; they were marshalled
with peculiar ceremonies, and odd rhapsodies were
preached over them.   The young clergyman of "a
noble" and prepossessing appearance, who could
preach so tenderly and dramatically, was exactly the
person for this "sensational" charity.   In that view,
no more judicious selection could have been made.
He was at first to work without any fixed salary. But
later in the following year, 1761, a "gratuity" of
sixty guineas was voted to the zealous advocate. The
year previous he had been only voted "thanks for
his many and great services."*   Not until 1763 was

---

* These and other extracts are from the MS. Registers of the Magdalen House.

he finally accepted as the regular chaplain, at a salary of one hundred guineas a year. The sermon which Mr. Dodd preached at the opening was printed in the following year, and was pronounced by the public press to be "a manly, rational, and pathetic address." To it was prefixed an account of the charity from the same hand, together with various "stirring" epistles from the reclaimed inmates to their relations, talking rapturously of "this blessed place," and the unspeakable happiness they enjoyed in putting on the peculiar garb of the establishment. And to add to the effect, the whole was enriched with an "elegant print of a young girl in her proper dress."

These fancies, directed, no doubt, by well-meaning views, were only appealing to that morbid curiosity which is dormant in every public of every age. Each Sunday the Magdalen was crowded, and crowded with "fashionables" of all degrees. But there was one special Sunday very famous in its annals—the Sunday when Prince Edward came; who, as he went about to every party in London, eager for excitement, was likely enough to be anxious to see the new entertainment in Goodman's-fields. For this occasion there were "great preparations"—the registers tell us.

People of fashion made parties to visit the Magdalen. Lady Northumberland was one of the early patrons of this charity; and at her house were pleasant and pious parties of pleasure made up of a Sunday, to go and hear this dramatic young clergyman preach over his Magdalens. On one occasion she could not attend, and her absence sent Doctor Dodd to his desk, to prepare "An Ode occasioned

by Lady N——d's being prevented by Illness from
coming to the Chapel of the Magdalen House." This
was shaped into the true lyrical fashion, commencing
with a burst:

> Hence loathed pain,
> With envious disappointment in thy train,
> But no more thy harpy hand
> Lay upon N——d.

In this ode he, as it were, advertises his Sunday's
entertainment, describing the "sensational" character
of what he had to show: with the

> Grateful songs and tuneful praise,
> *Pious orgies,* sacred lays:
> Finer pleasures which dispense
> Than the finest joys of sense.
> And each melting bosom move,
> And each liquid eye o'erflow
> With benevolence and love.

But one of the best passages in the Walpole letters
is the description of one of these pious Sunday junketings:

"Jan. 27, 1760.—Met at Northumberland H. at 5,
and four coaches. Prince Edward, Lady Mary Coke,
Lady Carlisle, Miss Pelham, Lady Hertford, Lord
Beauchamp, Lord Huntingdon, old Bowman, &c. . . .

"This new convent is beyond Goodman's-fields,
and would, I assure you, content any Catholic alive.
We were received by—oh! first a vast mob, for
princes are not so common at that end of the town as
at this. Lord Hertford, at the head of the governors,
with their white staves, met us at the door, and led
the prince directly into the chapel, where, before the

altar, was an arm-chair for him, with a blue damask
cushion, a prie-dieu, and a footstool of black cloth
with gold nails. We sat on forms near him. There
were Lord and Lady Dartmouth, in the odour of
devotion, and many city ladies. The chapel is small
and low, but neat; hung with Gothic paper and
tablets of benefactions; at the west end were enclosed
the sisterhood, above one hundred and thirty, all in
greyish-brown stuffs, broad handkerchiefs, and flat
straw hats, with a blue ribbon, pulled quite over
their faces. As soon as we entered the chapel, the
organ played, and the Magdalens sung a hymn in
parts; you cannot imagine how well. . . . . Prayers
then began, psalms, and a sermon; the latter *by a
young clergyman, one Dodd*, who contributed to the
Popish idea one had imbibed, by haranguing entirely
in the French style, and very *eloquently and touch-
ingly*. He apostrophised the lost sheep, who sobbed
and cried from their souls; so did my Lady Hertford and Fanny Pelham, till, I believe, the city dames
took them for Jane Shores. . . . . The confessor
then turned to the audience, and addressed himself to
his royal highness. . . . . In short, it was a very
pleasing performance, and I got the most illustrious
to desire it might be printed.

"From thence we went to the refectory, where all
the nuns without their hats were ranged at the tables
ready for supper. A few were handsome. I
was struck and pleased with the modesty of two of
them, who swooned away with the confusion of being
stared at."

On the occasion of this remarkable visit, the

preacher found opportunity to observe that conspicuous sensibility of Lady Hertford, which Walpole
himself had noticed, and at once embalmed it in—an
ode!—"Verses occasioned by Seeing the Countess of
Hertford in Tears at the Magdalen House"—with a
note, in which he took care to put on record that
"Prince Edward was in the chapel at the same time,
with several other (*sic*) of the nobility."

In these verses "Britain's GENIUS" saw the
Countess at the chapel, and mistook her for Charity.
There she saw

> The tender tears in plenty flow,
> Tears drawn by pity and by you,
> From her fair eyes.
>
> .　　.　　.　　.
>
> I know her well (the Grace rejoin'd),
> My sister, Pity, form'd her mind:
> She long has our familiar been:
> —'Tis H——'s countess that you mean.
> I know the place—the time I know,
> —'*Twas at my favourite house below.*

It seems surprising how such offensive adulation
could have been accepted.

"Pious orgies"—the words of Dodd himself—
would seem to have been about the best description
of this singular exhibition.

Some ten years later, the lively Doctor Carlyle
came up to London from Edinburgh—one of those
expeditions in which he used to combine private
business and pleasure, with some public interest of
the Scottish clergy. On this occasion, while battling
against the "Window-tax," which was in some way
affecting their interests, he went out into gay London

life, and seeing everything that was in fashion, found
his way of a Sunday to the Magdalen. The crowd of
" genteel people" was so great that it was with the
greatest difficulty that he found a seat.   Looking up,
he saw all the Magdalens exhibited in a gallery behind a very open lattice; " so that those," he says,
" who chose to be seen might easily effect that
object." The preacher then gave out his text—a
very unbecoming one for the place and occasion*—
and proceeded to deliver what Carlyle calls " a shock-
ing sermon," treating his subject with a bold inde-
licacy and detail, as, indeed, seems only too probable.
For this grossness, veiled under fashionable piety,
would appear to have been one of the sensational
attractions of the affair.   The Scotch clergyman even
remarked that some of the penitents were quite confused and agitated by this blunt handling of their
condition; but it is more likely that he mistook these
cries and sobbings of " the lost sheep"—which came
in at the proper place during the preacher's discourse,
and which Walpole had noticed—for symptoms of
shame and confusion.   They had been accustomed to
Doctor Dodd for some ten years, and it does seem
improbable that persons of their class would be so
affected.   During the discourse, " unceasing" mur-
murings of applause from the " genteel persons" were
going on all round him, which the Scotch minister,
who was not at all straitlaced for one of his cloth,
and went about merrily to parties and theatres, " con-
tradicted aloud."   With great warmth he condemned
the whole institution—at least the Sunday exhibition

---

* " If a man look on a woman," &c.

portion—"as *contra bonos mores,* and a disgrace to a Christian country."

It was not surprising that, besides the Scotch clergyman, there should be others who protested against the whole system, as unprofitable, and dangerous in its results, as a cruel and unbecoming exhibition, and who even hinted their suspicions as to the motives of the Conductor. Against these cavillers the Doctor was always in protest, and denounced them vigorously, even in his "Ode to Lady Northumberland:"

> Let the roving talkers boast,
> Who themselves to virtue lost,
>   Still seducing,
>   Still deluding,
> With ungrateful scoffs decry
> Those they won to wanton joy.
> All their censure to disprove,
> Let them seek this first retreat
> Britons gave to them whose love,
> Gives to life its choicest sweet,
> Then will they view it with abashed surprise
> *By ruin'd, but returning fair ones thronged.* *

Almost a small congregation might be formed of those who have heard him preach and left their impressions on record. Curwen, an American loyalist divine, was at the Magdalen on a Sunday in May, 1776—only a year before the final catastrophe—and the entry in his diary is highly characteristic. It shows the sort of text the Doctor loved to amplify, and also the way in which he affected the common run of hearers. "Heard the Reverend Doctor Dodd," he writes, "preach from John xv. 17: 'These things

---

* The comic circumlocution in the last line is almost without a parallel.

I command you, that ye love one another.' A most
elegant, sensible, serious, and pathetic discourse,
enough to have warmed a heart not callous to the
impressions of pity. I own my eyes flowed with
tears of compassion."

The loyalist was of those who follow what the
world follows. Only nine months later, the same
hand made another entry, with an amusing forgetfulness of the " elegant, sensible, and pathetic discourse,"
and of the tears of compassion which he himself had
shed. " A reverend," says the American, " known
by the name of the Macaroni Doctor, is in the Poultry
Compter for forgery. . . . *His real name Dodd.*
He figures in the *tête-à-têtes* in the Magazines, and,
unless defamed, is a worthless character, though noted
for some serious publications in the common routine.
He has two chapels and the Magdalen under his care."

This forgetfulness is charming, but only truly
typical of the class of the Doctor's admirers and
friends.

When John Taylor went to hear him, he found
that another clergyman had been obliged to take his
place, and had actually commenced the sermon when
the Doctor arrived. The clergyman at once stopped
and gave way to Dodd. Taylor remarked the energy
in his manner, and the theatrical nature of his ges-
tures and language. He had often seen him in the
street, stepping along in a stately manner, with his
head in the air, with no doubt the silk gown rustling
and flapping behind him.

CHAPTER THE SIXTH.

DODD "ON DEATH."

STILL at West Ham, he began to add a little to his
income by taking a few young gentlemen as pupils—
a practice he continued all his life. The year he
published his Magdalen sermon he became the Reverend William Dodd, M.A.; and the following year
presented the world with three volumes of Bishop
Hall's works. A more inappropriate editor for such
a book, or one less capable of apprehending the quaint
language and rare "conceits" of this old writer, could
not be well conceived. Sterne, on whom the eyes of
the town were then resting, knew and relished—and
even appropriated—the old divine far better. But
even in this bit of task-work the editor could not
steer clear of what was "unsound" and unwholesome.

With Secker, Archbishop of Canterbury—whom
Walpole has described—was living a relation, Miss
Talbot, and Dodd had introduced his book with
an epistle to this lady, full of servile flatteries of the
archbishop. "More especially," ran this fulsome
panegyric, " as you live remarkably blest in having

daily before your eyes a lively copy of piety as ex-
alted, sanctity as unaffected, and labour as unwearied,
as shone in the life of good Bishop Hall." The archbishop heard of this intended exaltation in good time,
and not relishing either the obligation, or, perhaps,
the ridicule, of such inflated praise (which, if we may
trust Walpole, he was far from deserving), insisted on
the sheet being cancelled. After a " warm expostu-
lation" this had to be done, and Mr. Dodd had the
mortification of having his panegyric rejected, and
what, perhaps, he felt more acutely, a profitable opening for patronage stopped up.

At every turn in the life of this "Macaroni Parson" we light on something thus awkward, "nasty,"
or at least suspicious.

From this sort of spasmodic range of subject, rush-
ing from Shakspeare to sermons, and from sermons
to odes, it seems as though the Reverend William
Dodd, M.A., was doing genteel sort of hack-work
for the booksellers. Still all these little engines
were bearing a steady profit. His name was getting
known, and he was attracting notice as one of those ·
dramatic clergymen who in every age attract a certain amount of attention and admiration. Next year
he sent out a book on Milton, and, a year later, the
well-known " Dodd on Death," perhaps the most
familiar to the public of all his writings. " First re-
tailed," said the *Monthly Review*, the " slashing" journal
of the day, " in the *Christian Magazine*, and now collected in a volume to frighten his Majesty's subjects
with dismal ideas of death, and horrible pictures of
damnation."

They were written, he tells us in the preface, with
the odd "design to be given away by *well-disposed
persons at funerals,* or on any other solemn occasion."
But the editors of a pious magazine induced him to
give them the first use of the papers. They are good
practical thoughts; perhaps a little too theatrical and
sensational, but likely to be useful to minds of a
certain order. Many of the most effective points
were, however, taken from Hervey, Young, Watts,
and others. He also introduced that round of characters which the essayists of the day were so fond of
using to point their moral—a whole crowd of Negotios,
Osianders, Misellas, Pulcherias, and others, who were
the regular *corps dramatique* of the *Ramblers* and
Guardians. In some of his illustrations there is a familiarity that almost borders on the Burlesque. In Negotio's instance, when " two more blisters were ordered to
six he already had upon him," we are not surprised to
hear that a " drowsy sleepiness, dire prognostic of death,
at length terminated in strong convulsions, and the busy,
active, sprightly Negotio died." In the character of
"Bubulo," he "improved" some City acquaintance who
"had incumbered for threescore and ten years the
earth with his heavy load, who had devoted hours to
his nice and enormous appetite. He was in this
respect a perfect animal."*

* One of the notes to Bubulo's history is truly Shandean:
" N.B.—A friend of the writer is pleased to observe: ' The " Reflections on Death" please me much. But don't you carry things rather
too far when you say, " 'tis an indispensable duty to go to our parish
church?" Was I to live in London, I should rarely or never go to my
parish church, if I had a *stupid, humdrum minister.* I long to live in

He also admitted into his collection a remonstrance made to poor Richard Nash, the M.C. of Bath, and which told that gentleman some very home truths. It is much to be suspected that it found admittance to the "Reflections" on the ground of their being written by Lady N——; of course, the same Lady N—— to whom he wrote the pleasant copy of verses on her not coming to the Magdalen. "I take my pen," said Lady N—— to Richard Nash, Esq., "to advise, nay, *to request of you*, to repent while you have an opportunity. . . . . I must tell you, sir, with the utmost freedom, that your present behaviour is not the way to reconcile yourself with God. . . . . Your example and your life is prejudicial—I wish I could not say fatal—to many. For this there is no amends but an alteration of your conduct *as signal and memorable as your person and name.*"

Doctor Dodd adds a comment on this statement which has a remarkable significance, and which I shall remind the reader of when I come to deal with the unfortunate clergyman's last declaration on the scaffold. "No man living," he says, in a note, "can have a higher regard for benevolence and humanity than the writer of these lines; . . . . as if *tenderness of heart*, and acts of charity, could atone for every other deficiency. It is hoped, therefore, that the writer of Nash's life will strike out that offensive and hurtful passage, wherever he asserts ' that there was nothing criminal in his (Nash's) con-

London, that I might hear clever men, &c. I disapprove, as much as you do, running after Methodist preachers and enthusiasts; but should I not prefer a Sherlock at the Temple, if I lived in Fleet-street ?' " &c. &c.

duct—that he was a harmless creature,' &c. And this is said of a man who, with a heart of exquisite humanity, was yet through life a gambler professed, and an encourager of illegal gambling!—a *follower of pleasure all his days, and a perpetual dissipator.*"

After their appearance in the *Christian Magazine,* these papers were collected into a little volume, enjoyed an immense popularity, and may have been actually distributed at funerals by the "well-disposed persons," as was intended by their author.

Gradually he came to conduct the *Christian Magazine* altogether; at least, his connexion with it was so intimate as to almost amount to conducting ; and it was said that the sermons of Doctor Dodd had been handsomely extolled by the very pen of Doctor Dodd himself. "His style," said this notice, "is at once elegant and nervous—neither careless nor yet affected —in short, such a style as we would recommend to the young divines who would desire to instruct without being tedious, and would *acquire popularity without meanness.*"

Perhaps among the most daring instances of effrontery, is his treatment in the same journal of another clergyman as gay as he was, but who, at least, did not make a livelihood out of a fashionable sanctity, and was honest enough to make no pretence of holiness. Sterne's Sermons sold better than Dodd's; in society, his gifts and fame quite eclipsed the Doctor's. But in oral sermons Dodd "drew" far better than Sterne, for at one Magdalen sermon the collection reached nearly fourteen hundred pounds; while the Reverend Mr. Sterne, with all his early popularity, with the bishops calling on him, and his

fortnightly dinners in advance—the *recherché* of states-
men, actors, and of all that was witty and fashionable—brought only some four hundred pounds to
the Foundling Hospital. Never was there such a
contrast between two men apparently so like. Both
were extravagant, both were shipwrecked by a craving
for society and amusement. But there was this difference: one was a pure hypocrite, and, what was
worse, found his profit in his hypocrisy: Sterne would
have scorned that sanctimonious trade. We know
no "dirty action" of his; and though often hard pressed
for money, he would never have dreamed of so dirty
an action as a forgery. All through, Mr. Sterne was
a gentleman. Conceive, then, the town speculator
in chapels-of-ease passing judgment on Yorick's Sermons in such words as these: "We are astonished
a man can deliver such sentiments, and act such a
life."* More surprising still was his remonstrance to
the popular author of "Tristram," on the publication
"of his third and fourth volumes :"

TO THE AUTHOR OF TRISTRAM SHANDY.

ON THE PUBLICATION OF HIS THIRD AND FOURTH VOLUMES.

Yes, they will laugh ;—but who, O S——e, inquire?
The wretched sons of vice and foul desire:
To these your page immoral may be dear,
But virtue o'er it sheds the conscious tear:
The wise, the modest, view it with concern ;
Detest the matter, and the master mourn.
   Is it for this you wear the sacred gown,
To write and live the Shandy of the town ?
Is it for this the holy hand was laid,
Thrice awful consecration !—on your head?

* This was in 1766.

D 2

Is it for this the sacred page was giv'n
To teach high truths, and point the way to heav'n?
Is it for this, that, trifler loose and vain,
With page unhallow'd, and with pen obscene,
You might against the cause of goodness war,
Soil the pure mind, and truth's fair features mar?
  Ah! think what you will surely know too soon,
Tho' some may laugh, none love the loose buffoon:
But of buffoons the scorn and veriest fellow,
Is the buffoon, strange monster—in prunello!
With all your might, tho' you have stretch'd your hand,
To scatter poison, and defile the land;
Yet let me once my gratulations pay,
For that your will exceeds your best essay:
I joy to praise you for your foulest sheet,
Jests most indelicate, and dearth of wit.
The time will come, when you with me shall join,
To bless the blasting of each putrid line:
For oh the time will come, when you shall feel
Stabs in your heart more sharp than stabs of steel:
When conscience loud shall thunder in your ear,
And all your wide-spread ill in horrid form appear!
  Prevent the hour, for pity's sake I ask,
And oh, perform your own advised task;*
Search your own heart, you'll find the debt is large,
And haste, perform the duties of your charge;
Leave the vile town, nor wish it in your pow'r,
To shine the giddy meteor of an hour.
Ah! you have talents,—do not misapply,
Ah! you have time,—seize, seize it, ere it fly;
Strait seize it, for too short you needs must own
Whate'er of life remaineth to atone
For all the filth diffus'd, and evil you have done.

It seems almost incomprehensible how such advice could come from one who was notoriously immersed in all the seductions of the vile town. But a habit of hypocrisy often induces a complacent self-delusion; and the actor, like Elliston playing in the Coronation, often takes himself to be what he is playing.

* See Sterne's Sermons, vol. i. Sermon fourth.

CHAPTER THE SEVENTH.

MARGATE.

In his summer junketings about this time, he seems to have had a liking for Margate. This partiality he ventilated with the same offensive ostentation that he did his other private tastes—his filial affection, and his conjugal regard for his wife. Society and parties at "The Rooms," and abundance of ladies to write verses to, were, with him, almost necessaries of life; and perhaps at Margate, whose sea-breezes were necessary after booksellers' task-work, he found these advantages most readily. A lady in London was naturally surprised at his choice of such a place, since it was believed in town that the lodgings were "mean, small, and base," and that the company who came down by the "hoy,"—perhaps of the same quality as Charles Lamb's fellow-passengers forty or fifty years later—was but of a sorry sort, and the whole not much above the level of a fishing village. But Mr. Dodd showed her presently in verses "Occasioned by a Lady's condemning," &c., that it was a most agreeable place, full of pleasant

company, and of carriages and horses.* To such attractions, however, he protests his indifference :

> Yet, Maria, yet, my fair,
> Happiness shall find us here,
> Happiness our friend shall be,
> *Ubiquarian* Deity.
>
> .   .   .   .
>
> Ha—Maria—then I've found
> Whence it comes that I am crown'd
> With such sweet serenity
> When accompanied by thee.

He then gives a picture of their walking together
"arm in arm upon the strand," talking of Clementina's
love, and of dropping a "tender tear" for that " pious
fair" who had just appeared in Sir Charles Grandi-
son—then riding over the "fertile isle," and winding
up in the evening with a visit to "The Rooms."

It is hard to find a reason for this constant thrusting of his conjugal affection on the public. His enemies would have accounted for it by an eagerness to
refute the popular rumours as to his morals and loose
habits. Something must be allowed for that phari-
saical affectation of pious domesticity and theatrical
virtue which is so plain in other parts of his life ;
but still he may be fairly credited with a certain
real affection for the verger's daughter, who was a
true wife, gently tolerant of his follies, and womanly
constant at the end.

He was deeply mixed up with all the pleasant and

---

* In a prose note, in defence of his watering-place, Dodd falls into
something like "a Bull." For he says: "The carriages and horses
are so numerous here, that there is not room enough for either : many
being obliged to send them to Ramsgate and elsewhere."

important trifling of the place. We almost see him acting as the adviser of the lively ladies in a little ball-room scene. One who greatly contributed to their "fun" and gaiety was "a gentleman whose beauty and address procured him the appellation of Cupid from the ladies two years ago," and who had acted as an amateur master of the ceremonies. Doctor Dodd knew his merits. He had seen him

Thro' the rooms advance,
Guide the gay band, and lead the sprightly dance.

This gentleman had directed the graceful minuet, chosen partners for the ladies, and

To the tuneful band with glove so white,
Could wave and bid them play each maid's delight.

He got partners and players in the card-rooms for "sober whist, brisk loo, or blithe quadrille." During the next visit of the Doctor, the loss of this useful person was sensibly felt:

Silent we sit, expecting who shall lead;
The music's silent—and the beaux seem dead;
Perchance a lonely minuet's begun,
But who shall dance the next when this is done?

The Doctor put this into his usual rhyming. He, too, appreciated the loss of this "Cupid" at "The Rooms," and, after his lively manner, slyly picked out a pretty lady, and put his poetical remonstrance into her mouth, as "Clorinde:"

Intrepid to the bath I once could hie,
For Love was there . . . . .
Now to that bath with timid step I go,
And plunge affrighted to the gulph below.

The Doctor knew well "Draper's," or "Nash-court," and was sometimes on " sober palfry," or " in coach drawn by *Margatian steeds*, much toiled, ill fed," and had often driven to see the Ramsgate pier, then in progress, " slow work of public cost." No wonder that, on quitting this pleasant spot where he had been so petted, he should feel regret, or that his heart should expand. Dwelling in a curiously mistaken spirit of prophecy on a picture of his end—blissful end—departing serenely and peacefully :

> So shall my weeping friends, when the last sigh
> Declares departed life, smiting their breasts,
> Say—" Lov'd he liv'd, and loving :—
> Peace to his shade,
> Embalm his memory, and receive him Heav'n !"

He little thought how many weeping friends, and yet more weeping spectators, were to be admitted to look on at his last moments.

During one of his visits, about the year 1762, he made an expedition from Margate to Brighthelmstone. He was one of a party, and they seem to have been very merry on the road, so much so that Doctor Dodd was induced to embody their pleasant adventures in his favourite vehicle, rhyme—and rhyme, too, of the usual quality. He must have lightened the way with true clerical jocularity. Looking back, as he wrote, the little ordinary incidents of an ordinary journey were quickened into events of a most exquisite humour,* though he hints that the notes were supplied by the company. At five o'clock on the first day they got to " Dull Sandwich," where they were welcomed by Lord ——, the warden of the Cinque

* This was not published until some years after his death.

Ports, who held the queen's canopy at the recent coronation, and who was now " so obliging" as to clothe himself in his coronation robes to entertain them.

> Mrs. ——, full of wonder sits,
> Admires the baron and his robes by fits.

The second day they came by moonlight

> Into dirty Deal,
> Where wretchedly we sup on fried-stewed veal.

A jocular note explains how this dish " was intended for cutlets, and then, it seemed, fried ; but it swam in so much sauce that we could conclude no less than that it was stewed." Then came Dover, and " smuggling, ill-built Folkstone," where they had excellent claret, of which

> We drank delighted, tho' we'd cause to fear
> That even claret pays no duty here.

Then they crossed the Romsey marshes, which, as the sands grow heavy, the horse of one of " our dear ladies" tripped and " fell ;" " fatal propensity in the female kind," adds the gallant clergyman.

On the third day they were at Rye, with which they were greatly pleased. " One of the party, a bookman, found out a bookseller," which would seem to point to the chronicler. Then came Winchelsea, where Mr. Norton treated them handsomely :

> Than Norton never man was more polite.

At Hastings they found bad entertainment, a drunken landlady, and " stinking beds."

A little farther, they passed the house of one of his

favourite pupils. " Ah, my lov'd Lancaster !" whom in a few years he was to apostrophise, in exactly the same words, from his cell in Newgate. Then, in a strange spirit of prophecy, which perhaps he thought would be merely dramatic in this place, but would not be so soon fulfilled, he added :

> Still toils thy friend thro' life's lone tedious way,
> But from thee hopes he has not long to stay;
> Quick on his journey passing soon he'll come,
> And joyful meet thee at our Father's home !

This little bit of pathos was no doubt only in harmony with the character he had been supporting during the journey ; the charming and diverting clergyman who put the little incidents in such a comic point of view, but who, every now and again, jumbled up some piety with his jocularity. These little hints which we gather from his writings, help wonderfully in the estimation of his character, which, as we go along, becomes perfectly clear and consistent.

CHAPTER THE EIGHTH.

STRUGGLES FOR PROMOTION.

HE was now well established as one of the " clever men," for whom the country friend, yearning after good preachers, would have quitted the parochial Fleet-street to listen to. The king, or more probably the Duke of Newcastle, put him in the list of Royal Chaplains; and about the same time he became acquainted with the Bishop of St. David's, Dr. Squire—a name that figures very frequently in the dedications of the period—a name, too, which wicked college undergraduates twisted into the more grotesque " Doctor Squirt." He was quite unknown to the bishop, but characteristically introduced himself by an admiring sonnet—a happy example of earnest heroics descending suddenly into burlesque. He sings him as addressing Religion and Reason:

> Attendant thereon, heavenly Reason came,
> And on Religion's shrine an offering laid;
> I saw it straight her whole attention claim;
> Then what it was I could not but *inquire.*

The reader is almost forewarned of the rhyme that is to follow :

Instant, with rapture,—" 'Tis my son's," she said,
"The polish'd page of *my judicious* SQUIRE !"

This dignitary took a fancy to young Mr. Dodd, just as the stormy Bishop of Gloucester had done to Mr. Sterne ; and, like that prelate, may have repented later of his hasty patronage. This swarthy bishop, known to the irreverent as "The Man of Angola," was so pleased with his *protégé* that he presented him to the prebend of Brecon, and favoured him in many other ways. One of the fair places in our clergyman's character is his gratitude to this bishop, which blossomed out in sonnets and dedications, and which— a far better test—was found green and healthy after Doctor Squire had laid down his mitre for ever. Any proclamation of favours received, when after the hand that has offered them can offer no more, is very often omitted, as unnecessary, and even troublesome homage. Even in his prison cell he thought of the old kindness, and paid a grateful tribute to the memory of his patron :

And bless'd by thee, St. David's ! honoured friend,
Alike in wisdom's and in learning's school
Advanc'd and sage ! Short pause, my muse, and sad,
Allow, while leaning on affection's arm,
Deep-sighing gratitude, with tears of truth,
Bedews the urn—the happy urn—where rest
Mingled thy ashes, oh, my friend ! and hers,
Whose life, bound up with thine in amity,
Indissolubly firm, felt thy last pang.

He also saluted him with an epigram, under the title

of " Gratitude and Merit," and allowed his poetic
fancy to take the form of " An Ode, written in the
Walks of Brecknock." All these *jade* shapes of compliment have, happily, had their day, and persons of
influence do not now care to have the sickly censers
of dedications and sonnets swung before them as they
walk. More genuine was his address to Mrs. Squire,
his widow, in his preface to a sermon, when he says
—" Alas, madam! we think with anxious concern of
the exquisite sensibility of his affectionate heart."
The wags of the day were pleasant on this subject,
and seemed to enjoy the Doctor's loss of his patron :

> Dodd bit his sacred lip that day,
> And furled his holy brow ;
> An arch-priest then was heard to say—
> " *Soho!* who'll *Squire* you now ?"

It has been said that it was through this influence
that the smooth Chesterfield, casting about for a suitable director of his nephew's education, was induced
to select the young Royal Chaplain. But Doctor
Dodd himself tells us that it was only " by the advice
of my dear friend, now in heaven, Doctor Squire,"
that he agreed to accept this office. It was, indeed,
an interruption to his preferment ; and we have only
to look into Sterne's sermons, and Goldsmith's essays,
to see into what disrepute the function had fallen.
It was only by " promises," no doubt, of suitable preferment that he was induced to " engage" for this
boy's education ; and it is quite characteristic of the
noble contractor that these promises remained " un-
fulfilled." The convict clergyman, looking back to
this stage of his life, bitterly complains of this treat-

ment, and half lays the beginning of his fall upon
this hollow patron :

> Sought by thee,
> And singled out, unpatronised, unknown ;
> By thee, whose taste consummate was applause,
> Whose approbation merit ; forth I came,
> And with me to the task, delighted, brought,
> The upright purpose.

It has been said that he went abroad with his pupil,
and took "the grand tour"—more necessary then for
a young person of quality than a university education ; but there are no evidences of such a journey
beyond a loose statement in the rude memoir of him
which remains. Little scraps of preferment were
now gradually tiding him on, and he would scarcely
have turned aside for so serious and prolonged an
interval. He was now entering fairly on his London
career.

Mr. Walpole had remarked the presence of many
"City people" at the strange Magdalen performance ;
and among this class, indeed, were to be found his
chief patrons and followers. It was through the influence of some "City people" that he was appointed
Chaplain to his Majesty. Foote, in his satire—to
be spoken of later—alluded to his frequent presence
at the great "City feasts ;" and at the last act of life,
a City alderman stood forward at his trial, and indi-
rectly strove to help him. London was now to be his
sphere. He had made ineffectual attempts to succeed
to the rectorship of West Ham ; but being twice disappointed, at last quitted the place. "A place," he
says, "ever dear, and ever regretted by me ;" and
dwells on the change very pathetically, since his life

there was pastoral, and full of pleasant country labour, now to be exchanged for London seductions. After his long service at West Ham, he was beginning to reckon on the reversion of the rectory as almost a certainty. Lord Hertford was the patron, and moreover a governor of the Magdalen, and Lady Hertford was among the listeners on the great "sensation" occasion described by Walpole. It came, therefore, with a shock on him, when Lord Hertford appointed his own chaplain—a dull Scotch clergyman, who once preached in the Ambassador's Chapel at Paris, and made Wilkes yawn, a few Sundays before Sterne preached from the same pulpit to all the wits and unbelievers in Paris. Later, this Scotch chaplain became, through the same interest, an Irish bishop, and once more the living was left vacant; but again the unlucky Dodd was disappointed. Soon, too, St. Olave's also became vacant, and the lecturer, who had been looking eagerly for the post, experienced another cruel reverse. He had dedicated to the Duke of Newcastle, and it was given to Dr. Owen, actually, "on the recommendation of the Duke of Newcastle." He was indeed indefatigable in hunting out openings for promotion. He tried a hundred different channels, and like most people who try a hundred different channels, he failed hopelessly. His wife's brother, Perkins, was well known to Sir John Hawkins, and was also his tenant, and from him the knight obtained some odd details about the Doctor's habits and manners. Perkins was always employed to carry notes, messages—in every shape of importunity, to all sorts of great and influential persons—soliciting promotion to all manner of vacant livings. So much so that the messenger, as he himself described it, often hardly escaped being kicked down stairs. The brother-in-law described him as living at an obscure corner of Hampstead Heath; but as living in a style of luxury utterly beyond his visible means.*

* Sir John Hawkins had also heard rumours of a far more discredit-able sort. See his " Life of Johnson."

CHAPTER THE NINTH.

"THE ROYAL CHAPLAIN."

As chaplain, he now had chambers in the palace; and, almost at the outset, the indiscreet chaplain's head gave way. Tea-parties were given under the royal roof, and a little scandal went round, that the divine received lady friends at these entertainments. This was no very heinous dereliction; but it showed that, in a worldly sense, young Mr. Dodd, like poor Yorick, "carried not one ounce of ballast." By-and-by, when it came to be his turn to perform the service, his approach was heralded by the "rustling of silk," and a general atmosphere of clergymanical dandyism, to the grievous confusion of "old Groves," the royal "Table-decker." These were straws; but they were significant straws.

The degree of M.A. was scarcely of sufficient glory for the Chaplain to his Majesty; so, in 1766, he went down to Cambridge, and came up the Reverend William Dodd, LL.D., and then he launched himself fairly upon town. He first stopped in Pall-Mall, the street where Mr. Sterne first stayed when *he* came up. He had, besides, a country house at Ealing; and,

E

where he had before kept a modest chariot, he now
burst forth in all the majesty of a coach. The excuse
for this extravagance was the benefit of his pupils,
who had now increased in number and quality. Besides young Stanhope, a youth of about ten or eleven
years old, he had a young boy named Ernst, to both
of whom he seems to have been attached. The latter
obtained a post in some foreign station; and long
after, the luckless Doctor looked back piteously to the
happy days when he was directing their studies :

> Ah! my lov'd household! ah, my little round
> Of social friends! well do you bear in mind
> Those pleasing evenings, when, on my return—
> Much wished return—serenity the mild,
> And cheerfulness the innocent, with me
> Entered the happy dwelling! Thou, my Ernst,
> Ingenuous youth, whose early spring bespoke
> Thy summer, as it is, with richest crops
> Luxuriant waving. Gentle youth, canst thou
> Those welcome hours forget?

To young Stanhope, too, he addressed a similar apostrophe, which, on the ground of the old connexion,
should have been more fruitful in result than "the
windage" of a mere burst of poetry :

> Or thou—O thou!
> How shall I utter from my beating heart,
> Thy name so musical, so heavenly sweet
> Once to these ears distracted! Stanhope, say
> Canst thou forget those hours when clothed in smiles
> Of fond respect, thou and thy friend have strove
> Whose little hands should readiest supply
> My willing wants—officious in your zeal
> To make the Sabbath evenings, like the day,
> A day of sweet composure to my soul?

The youth who bore the " name so musical, so heavenly

sweet," and who was so dutiful in the little household, was later to stand up in a crowded court, and convict his tutor of an offence for which the penalty was death.

When the Magdalen Society was getting its rules into shape, it was thought advisable to have royal patronage, and accordingly the secretary and treasurer, with the Reverend Doctor Dodd, waited on her Majesty with the rules; on which she allowed herself to be named "Patroness" of the Institution.* Later on he edited the hymns and prayers for the use of the society, and this production was "submitted" to Bishop Porteous for approbation.†

He had now moved to Southampton-row, Bloomsbury; was writing in the *Public Ledger*, where he was allowed to spread his adulation of his patron, Doctor Squire, with a broad trowel. In that journal he published the "Visitor," a sort of weekly essay, afterwards gathered up into a two-volume sheaf; and was receiving a hundred a year for what he contributed to the pious *Christian Magazine*. Of that journal he was now, or a little later, sole editor. He was getting ready a new edition of "Locke's Common-Place Book"—for his name brought money to the booksellers. But so dramatic a preacher should surely have a house of his own; and the young Doctor, without a living, and who appealed at spasmodic intervals for a charity, ought to have had a private stage for himself. A curious circumstance, which occurred about this time, might be said to have suggested the idea.

* MS. Registers.   † Ibid.

E 2

Mrs. Dodd, the verger's daughter—though penniless when she married—obtained a sort of accidental dowry later. A lady, to whom she had been a kind of companion, left her one thousand five hundred pounds when she died, which was supplemented by another fortuitous contribution. Mrs. Dodd was at an auction, when a cabinet was put up, for which she began to bid. A lady of quality was also anxious to secure it; and when Mrs. Dodd discovered who was her opponent, she made a low courtesy, and withdrew. The lady of quality—possibly as frantic as Goldsmith's "old deaf dowager," at the auction which Mrs. Croker had been attending—was so pleased with this forbearance, that she came up to her, and begged the pleasure of a better acquaintance. The better acquaintance produced this fruit—that shortly after the grateful lady presented her with a lottery ticket, which, on being drawn, came out a prize of one thousand pounds.

This windfall our Doctor wisely determined to lay out in erecting a little private temple for his own performances. He entered into a sort of partnership with a builder; a plot of ground was secured in Pimlico, profitably close to the royal palace; and very shortly a chapel-of-ease rose, to which was given the name of Charlotte Chapel, in compliment to the reigning queen. He had great expectations from this pious speculation—for speculation it was; and it became, as might be imagined, a fashionable Sunday place of prayer. Four pews were set apart for the queen and her household. He had a highly fashionable congregation:

Pleasing, persuasive Patterns—*Athole's* Duke,
The polished *Hervey*, *Kingston* the humane,
Aylesbury and *Marchmont*, *Romvey* all revered,

as he could pompously enumerate them, thinking over his Court Calendar when he lay under sentence of death in Newgate. The sermons of the Reverend Doctor became very popular, and Nichols, the indefatigable gleaner of anecdotes, who often went to hear him preach, says he listened to him with delight.

By a sort of hereditary infamy, this chapel passed, within the memory of the present generation, to another occupant of the same tone and manners as the unlucky founder, and whose career, though ending not so fatally, was to the full as discreditable.

Here he was fortunate enough to light on a useful clerical assistant, the Reverend Weedon Butler, who, from this time until the death of the luckless proprietor of the Pimlico chapel, clung to him through all his fortunes; and it is one of the redeeming circumstances in this strange character that he was able to attach, at least, this one faithful heart. This was a young man whom he "took up" to be his amanuensis and general assistant in his literary work. He was originally intended for the law, but was induced by his patron to go into the church; and when the new chapel was opened, he became the reader, and alternate celebrant with Doctor Dodd. He had a brother, who was captain of the *William Pitt*, "extra" East Indiaman, which ship "foundered with all her crew, during a tremendous gale at midnight, off Algoa-Bay, after firing several half-minute signal-guns." He "reached the goal of immortality before his elder brother," said an obituary notice of the day.

The new chapel was in such vogue, that every sitting was soon disposed of. In fact, a dissatisfied Mr. Cookfield wrote up to the Doctor's friend from Upton, that he was " sorry that no seats were allotted to those whom *curiosity* or devotion brings to the chapel" (it was scarcely the latter that brought Mr. Walpole and party). " Some pews," continues the country gentleman with severity, " are occupied by only one or two persons ; but if the learned divine, instead of thinking to gain by godliness, were to believe his godliness gain, *many parts of his conduct would be different*—he would thus silence many who watch him with evil eyes. The Doctor would think me impertinent or a fool if I was to give him personally this very just bit of advice." The truth was, the Doctor was not responsible for the empty pews, which no one durst enter; for the concern being a speculation, the seats had gradually become the property of parties in the parish, who, when the novelty wore off, became, at least as far as their sittings were concerned, piously selfish—not coming themselves, nor yet allowing others to come.

There was a chapel also in Charlotte-street, Bloomsbury, and here too he joined in a sort of clerical partnership with a Doctor Trussler. With these fields of labour open to him, he seems to have been really indefatigable. He preached every Sunday morning at the Magdalen, while his brother and Mr. Butler took the evening duty at Pimlico, alternately. Nor were his literary labours abating. He was busy with all manner of schemes ; and foremost among these were his plans for a huge commentary on the Bible : a task which embodied the very ideal of pure drudgery

and hodman's labour—the weariest fetching and
carrying of the bricks and stones of erudition—not
even of the character, half light, half flashy, which,
with men of the world, counterbalance the labour they
bring to such a duty.

In fact, his was a most curious shape of character
—almost a puzzle for its hostile elements. Never
was the truth, that mere piety—that is, a taste for
praying—standing by itself, may be, after all, but
one of the many fancies of the human soul. All the
time that the Reverend Doctor Dodd was preaching
at St. James's, at the two Charlotte Chapels, and at the
Magdalen, and also busily working up his commentary on the Bible, and edifying friends by his delightful conversation on divine things, we may be curious
to know how this holy man was, as it were, filling in
his inner life. There is no need of any uncharitable
speculation, for he himself tells us:

" Thus brought to town and introduced to gay life,
I fell into snares. Besides this, the habit of uniform
regular piety and devotion wearing off, I was not, as
at West Ham, *the innocent man* I lived there. I committed offences against my God, which I bless Him
were always in reflection detestable to me. . . . Indeed, before I never dissipated at all—for many, many
years never seeing the playhouse, nor any public
place."

Allowing all charitable sincerity to this declaration,
there is still a disagreeable unctuousness about it, a
sort of indistinct complacency, which suggests the
" terrible example." He was indeed all the while a
whitened sepulchre.

CHAPTER THE TENTH.

DRAWING-ROOM VERSES.

THE keeping of the coach, the banqueting with City friends, and the country-house at Ealing, involved him in serious expenses. Money had to be found, and he tells us that he " fell into the ruinous mode of raising moneys by annuities. *The annuities devoured me,*" it is added, in a forcible expression which came not from him, but from the manly hand of Johnson. And yet, it was said that his Pimlico chapel brought him in some six hundred pounds a year.

Presently came forth a neat, pleasant collection of the agreeable clergyman's poems—lively, fashionable trifles, which were bought by the " City ladies," and found on the drawing-room tables on the other side of Temple Bar.

From this little Book of Poems—first collected in 1767—we can put together a picture of the drawing-room parson, dangling after ladies, eager to adorn every boudoir adventure with some trifling *vers d'occasion.* We can almost see him at " The Rooms," in his " full-bottomed wig " and " rustling silks," stooping over some of his "favourite fair," "rallying" them agreeably, quarrelling delightfully, and comforting them with compliments to their beauty and sweet religious thoughts alternately; and, finally, sending them home in the expectance of a poetical *billet-doux* next morning from the charming Doctor.

These effusions would have suited the professional beau, or a French gallant, more than an English clergyman. Thus was written "An Ode occasioned by a young Lady's laughing at me for staying from an Assembly," which winds up in this fashion :

> Soon the scene my soul alarming,
>   Came that Cupid* and his train,
> And a Venus, Delia, believe me,
>   Fair and form'd in stamp like thine.
> Cupid's whispers can't deceive me,
>   Both are sisters, both divine.

The gallant clergyman thus paints his feelings at this "staying from an assembly :"

> Cytherea fond attending,
>   Wou'd young Paris not have gone ?
> You, with beauty hers transcending,
>   Sighing, view'd I, forc'd to shun.

Lines scarcely smooth enough for the drawing-room ; and hardly so airy as the lines "Occasioned by the same young Lady's refusing to play at Quadrille when asked by a Gentleman," who, of course, stands for the agreeable Doctor Dodd :

> The queen was fainting, "Hartshorn, pray."
> All the choice spirits in a hurry,
> The ladies too in such a flurry :
> O shocking! what can all this bring ?
> "Haste—salts, drops, spirits—anything !"

* "Miss P.'s brother, a little boy about three years old."

He represents this young lady, "Miss Mat," as refusing to obey the "queen of quadrille" at a fashionable rout, and breaking out into a sort of coquettish
rebellion :

> Lo, a fair nymph refus'd to play,
> Nay, and what more the crime completed,
> Tho' by a gentleman intreated!
> Putting the rest in fear and fret
> Of that day making up a set.
> —Punish such presumptuous beauty,
> That others hence may know their duty.

When some of the company disparage the charms
of this lady with

> ——stuff, mere stuff! Pha! Bagatelle!
> Nonsense! But pray to know her better,
> Describe this beauty—La poor creature!

Which furnishes Doctor Dodd with an opening for
skilfully insinuating compliments :

> ——tho' her eyes are sweetly bright,
> And would kill thousands, if they might:
> She keeps them modestly at home,
> Nor lets their pointed ogles roam.

In the same key is "The Apology," addressed to
"Miss I——t," which begins,

> Break my word, sweet nymph, with thee!

which was followed by "A Second Apology" to the
same lady, who had accused him of flattery in the
first. He justifies himself in this jingle :

> Very blind, my dear I——t, needs must you be,
> Not the charms of your elegant person to see.

And he bids her

> Remember, fair daughter of softest delight,
> The chat which we held in the Rooms t'other night.

And in this he mixed up some piety with his compliments, according to the old and approved receipt, for this jumble of gallantry and spirituality has long been the conventional equipment of clergymen of that pattern. "Miss F——r," a friend of his wife, received an address, beginning;

> When I think, my dear F——, how rarely we find
> For friendship all proper endowments of mind.

So with the ode "To Two agreeable Sisters," one of whom was named Eliza; and with an effusion called "Suspense; written while waiting for the coming of a Lady," in which he thus chides the lingering moments:

> Since I held her hand—vexation,
>   Thrice ten hundred minutes pass'd!
> Come, my love, my charmer, bless me!
>
>   .   .   .   .
>
> Little rebel, I'll subdue thee.

In which occurs a wonderful apostrophe to a watch, the unconscious burlesque of which is exquisite:

> Watch! thou dotard time, more faster—
> But one hour—I thought it four!
> Dull machine—*unlike thy master,*
>   *Clicking even ever more!*

Allowing some margin for the elaborate gallantries of the day, it is impossible not to feel contempt for

this trifling. "Little rebel, I'll subdue thee," was
childish on lips that were the next evening to deal
with the grave truths of the Gospel. And though an
extempore sonnet might seem harmless enough, still
the *publishing* of such trifling, with the name of "the
great Doctor Dodd" attached, shows a want of self-
respect that nothing can extenuate.

A young lady, "Miss Jackson of Southgate," was
distinguished by his admiration, and he celebrates her
attractions in several of his effusions. She presented
him with a rosebud, which, almost of course, entailed
the unfailing return of " Verses occasioned by a Present of a Moss-Rosebud, &c.," in which, according to
his old pattern, were mixed up a little gallantry and a
little pretty piety. After telling her that the rose's
bloom " is but dull to her check's blushing tint," and
that, compared with her touch, "hard and rough is
the cygnet's most delicate down," he introduces the
moral :

> Remember a virtue the rose hath to boast—
> Its fragrance remains when its beauties are lost.

The same lady's name occurs incidentally in others of
his verses :

> Each steals a J—k—n's or a Booth's form.

In short, this collection betrays the Doctor in a
hundred little attitudes of drawing-room gallantry :
whether as " Listening to a young Lady singing
Spenser's Amoretti;" or as consoling " Mr. J——
on the Report of Miss ——'s Marriage;" or as whis-
pering to "A Friend in the Army" about " Kitty

Carr;" or as sympathising with the gentleman who was distracted by the charms of "Patsy," one of the "two agreeable sisters;" or as taking "lovely W——'s hand" in his; or as singing "Belinda," "Clorinda," "Eliza," and many more at whose feet the agreeable clergyman sat.

If we consider the little adventures these rhymes stand for—the playful quarrels at "The Rooms" with cruel and pretty ladies, the reconciliation, as playful, and the Doctor sitting down the next day to turn his verses, which were to be followed up by other "Apologies," it will be found that the whole represents an amount of trifling and philandering which no clergyman who had a sense of the decencies owing to his profession could have indulged in, or found time for. In the tone of these gallantries there is something almost offensive, and they unhappily help to fill in that popular portrait of the "Macaroni Parson" by which he is best known.

Even in his advertisement, written from Southampton-row, February 14, 1767, there is an ostentatious blazoning of filial virtue almost suspicious. In this he affects a sort of reluctance to bring his pieces before the public, and would not have done so, but rather that "he is thus enabled to pay a debt of filial affection," which was thus discharged in the dedication :

TO THE MEMORY

OF THE

REVEREND WILLIAM DODD, M.A.,

MANY YEARS VICAR OF BOURN IN LINCOLNSHIRE;

WHO DIED AUGUST 8, 1756,

AGED 54 :

AND OF ELIZABETH HIS WIFE,

WHO DIED MAY THE 21ST, 1755,

AGED 55.

WORTHY PARENTS,

WHOSE PARTIAL FONDNESS ENCOURAGED,

BUT WHOSE WISE, SOLICITOUS, AND EVER-VALUED CARE

ENABLED THEIR SON TO FAR BETTER PURSUITS,

THAN "THIS IDLE TRADE:"

THAT SON,

WITH THE HIGHEST FILIAL VENERATION,

INSCRIBES THIS LITTLE VOLUME OF POEMS,

AS AN HUMBLE, BUT AFFECTIONATE MONUMENT OF

THEIR MERIT, AND OF HIS LOVE.

BEST OF PARENTS !

WE SHALL MEET AGAIN !

The gem of the whole, unmatched, it would almost seem, for its cool effrontery and defiance of public report, is the motto chosen from Cicero's Archias :

"Merely the time that others find for unsuitable feasts, for play, and for amusements, *I* have set aside for the cultivation of these tastes."

This proclamation, it must be borne in mind, being made at a season when it was notorious that far more time than others would have found for verses, he was wasting in convivial dinners and suppers, in play, and in amusement. As compositions, too, they were of the poorest quality, even in days when feeble and meaningless verses of society of poorest quality were in vogue; and even from the specimens given it will be seen with what a comic clumsiness they were turned, and with what vapid nonsense they were filled. No wonder that the monthly reviewers should dismiss it contemptuously in three lines: saying that the worst thing they would say in favour of these poems is their author's youth, and the best, that they were beautifully printed by Leach.

CHAPTER THE ELEVENTH.

THE " CITY DINNERS."

THE commentary, too, was getting forward; but Weedon Butler, the faithful secretary, amanuensis, and man of all work, was behind the scenes, doing a good deal of the mere navvy's work. And even in this task broke out some of the false copper metal through the outside plating; and much of that flash and trickery, which, either in true shape or by suspicion, hung about all his life and labour. For he announced with a flourish that he was to have the use of papers and notes left by John Locke, and also some notes of Cudworth, which were in Lord Masham's hands.* And yet it was insinuated at the time that he knew well that these documents were either spurious, or not forthcoming. As the king's chaplain passed by in his "rustling silk," men looked after

---

* These papers he announced as including interleaved Bibles of Locke and Waterland, " with a curious MSS. of Lord Clarendon, written in his own hand." For more about this matter, see the article on Chillingworth, in Chalmers.

him, and admired (though it was said that he had
turned vain and "pompous," and was puffed up);
but still there was an impression as of something unsound, which would be discovered later.

There were many who believed in him. The
faithful Weedon Butler held to him through all.
While the Doctor was being eaten up with the dreadful annuities, and plunging deeper into the town delights, which the annuities went to purchase, the
trusty henchman did what he could to aid him.
Weedon Butler kept a diary, and we look over his
shoulder on the 23rd of March, 1787, as he writes:
" Engaged all the evening with Doctor Dodd, in trans-
lating Bishop Lowth's Lectures." And in the following month we see a more significant entry: " Did
not go out all day; *the Doctor abroad;* when he
returned in the evening, sat down with him to Bishop
Lowth's Lectures." Later, the too partial clerk wrote
to a friend: " I think I see every day more and more
the benefits derived to myself from Doctor Dodd."
Even a young American clergyman wrote over, in a
transport of pious desire, that he longed for nothing
so much in this world as to see the Doctor bishop of
" that quarter of the globe"—a pastoral charge too extensive, certainly, for one man, and as a sphere of
missionary action wholly unsuited to the Magdalen
preacher's tastes. We have a little after-dinner picture, when Doctor Dodd had Mr. Hoole to meet
Hawksworth, the translator of Telemachus; and the
subject of the divine government of events being
started, the Doctor turned his chair towards the fire-
place, and " *looking down to the fender,* spoke slowly

F

and gently, in an uninterrupted strain that delighted all. No one replied."

We can see the Doctor at one of the little City dinners, driving there in his carriage. The Messrs. Dilly of the Poultry—and readers of Boswell know of many pleasant dinners at that house—gave a party in the November of this year, to Wilkes, Mr. Jones, afterwards Sir William, De Lolme of the "English Constitution," Doctor Dodd, Sir Nathaniel Wraxall—whose accuracy, often impeached in the pleasant epigram "misquoting facts all," is daily more and more established by independent evidence—and two or three more. Johnson had met Wilkes at a little dinner— one of the most delightful in Boswell—at the same house a few months previously. Wraxall knew Dodd very well. The party was "gay, animated, and convivial," so much so, that Doctor Dodd invited the whole party to dine with him in Argyle-street on an early day. To Wraxall he was particularly attentive, and on going home set him down at the St. James's Coffee-house. The baronet, who was a man of the world, and a good judge of a man of the world, always found him "plausible and agreeable, lively, entertaining, and well informed."

The dinner he gave to Messrs. Dilly's party was an elegant repast, and Wraxall remarked the "French wines of various sorts." Mrs. Dodd "presided," and in the evening received a large company of friends. This is all characteristic—the inviting of the party en masse from the house where he was dining, and the evening entertainment got up so suddenly, while all this time the "lively, entertaining" host was "devoured by annuities;" the carriage that set the baronet down, the elegant repast, and the French wines not paid for, and actually a bill of sale on the seat where Mrs. Dodd "presided!" This is the last glimpse we have of the Doctor in society.

With this little vista of pastoral innocence, the decent, respectable portion of the Doctor's life fades out; and it makes a very curious study to see how gradually the furies of extravagance, pleasure, and the other familiars of gay life, preying on his weak, unfortified nature, gradually dragged him down to destruction.

BOOK THE SECOND.

THE "MACARONI PARSON."

CHAPTER THE FIRST.

"CITY FEASTING."

STILL, though so pleasant an after-dinner impression was left on Mr. Hoole, there was a growing belief abroad that something was wrong. The extravagance, the entertaining of the "noble pupils," and the City feasting, were spoken of openly; but in that day public opinion in reference to the cloth was in a state of utter unsoundness, and so far from attempting to check, seemed rather to encourage a degraded tone among the men who wore the gown. A coarse jest, or a broad scoff, was, at most, the only reproof uttered by the lax society of "fine" ladies and gentlemen of the time. A popular print of him about this time is in itself significant—for it exhibits him a smooth, smirking, full-length—in a studied attitude, dressed, not in gown and bands, but in a richly flowered dressing-gown and elegant smalls, while one ruffled hand rests ostentatiously on a tremendous volume, which may be assumed to represent his Bible Commentary.

One of Dodd's most faithful friends, who did not desert him in his extremity, Governor Thicknesse, speaking of him with good-humoured, but disrespectful familiarity, owns he " was as good and pleasant a tempered rascal as ever lived, or ever was hanged;" and gives him such commendation as one would give to a free, jovial, easy-mannered friend, who was amusing, but not very strict in principle. " An excellent companion," says Governor Thicknesse, " when he fell into such company he *could trust*, as he called it. I have heard him often making all the old women cry at church in the morning, and make his trusty friends laugh as much in the evening, with his song of Adam and Eve on

> Stopping in the Land of Nod
> To have their horses shod."

It was known, too, that the gay divine was in the habit of frequenting a tavern with his wife, and dining there " *tête-à-tête* in the most voluptuous manner;" and afterwards, on the very same day, would sup at a second tavern in the same style. These were not heinous transgressions in themselves: but they are sure marks and tokens, which the skilful in reading character and moral descent can readily interpret, as significant of more fatal delinquency.

He tried every way to bring himself notoriety, and then preferment. He even attempted to force his way into the famous Literary Club; but his overtures were received with significant coldness. "It would not have done," said Johnson, "that one of our club should have been hanged; not but," he added, smiling, "that some of them *deserved it;*" alluding pleasantly to Burke's wild French dreams. If he had been admitted, he could not have long remained a member, for the great spirit of the place would soon have pierced through the flimsy disguise and exposed him.

To Horace Walpole, who disliked him as he did the bishops, and as he did Sterne, had drifted some stories, which he set down in certain entries in his recently published diary. His pen is sharper, and his ink mixed with more gall than usual, as he deals with the luckless Doctor. He raked into his *chiffonnier's* scandal-basket some doubtful stories — that Mary Perkins, the verger's daughter, had been a handsome woman, for whom Lord Sandwich had been anxious to provide. She had an incurable passion for drink, which the Doctor encouraged, in order that he might have opportunity of the evening to go forth upon town, and entertain himself in his own way without hindrance. The same authority found out and jotted down an uncharitable remark of Bishop Newton, when the Doctor was in his last sore distress. "I am sorry for him," said the prelate. Some one asked, "Why?" "Because he is to suffer for the least of all his offences." The behaviour of Mrs. Dodd all through her husband's dreadful probation, and his testimony to her merits, does not square with Walpole's bit of scandal. Yet, true or untrue, the town were in possession of these stories.

Whether he feasted at taverns or not, he was still busy, at what might be called his religious hack-work, for the booksellers. Presently came out the huge three volumes of sermons to the young men, which were dedicated to his pupils, young Stanhope and Ernst. On which followed his translation of sermons from Massillon, and other " job-work" of the same order. It was, indeed, no other than job-work, and he and his faithful Weedon Butler laboured at this duty with great industry. His name was in good esteem with the booksellers.

The youths whom he was educating became useful in one sense, for they were young men of fortune and quality, and were to see London life, and yet could not do so without the care of their " governor." Chancellor Hoadly, another free clergyman, was at a great masquerade given in September, 1771—a crowded affair, though the supper was of poor quality. He saw " the great Doctor Dodd" there with his pupils, flaunting by decorated with jewels of silver. " The great Doctor Dodd" was Hoadly's ironical estimate of the public ideal. But he also represented the freer sceptics, who did not accept the pious character of the Doctor. " He was there," he says, " merely, *I suppose*, to look after his two youths. I wish somebody had placed two or three of his Magdalens upon him. It would have been a good and new character." Hoadly himself made no affectation of purism, and was free of the Stage and the Actors' Corporation.

All the stories about him, however we may suspect

them to have been coloured up by mistake or prejudice, have a certain "Dodd"-like savour, quite in harmony with his life. Thus, when the "young lady of fortune in the City" told Mrs. Dodd certain rumours some one had been circulating about her (Mrs. Dodd's) character—and when the Doctor, having received fifty pounds as compensation under threat of a prosecution, handed it over pompously to his charity as having been "paid for a defamation"—it is difficult not to accept this flourish, it is so characteristic. What the shape of this "defamation" was, Horace Walpole had heard, as well as the young lady of fortune.

The translation of some of Massillon's Sermons had possibly recommended itself to him as likely to be good matter for "Court Sermons." But Scott, the well-known "Anti-Sejanus," was watching him. Anti-Sejanus was in the pay of the abandoned Lord Sandwich, and perhaps recollected how his patron had been introduced into the Doctor's novel. He flung himself on him, and publicly gibbeted him in these bitter lines:

> Meek, humble, modest parson Dodd,
> Believe me, it is mighty odd,
>   That you such hopes should dish up;
> For after all, my good friend Will,
> Whate'er you think, you will be still
>   A priest, but not a bishop.
>
> The parties which you tried to fix
> Of ladies (monstrous thus to mix !),
>   To grace the chaplain's table;
> Carnal with spiritual thus to join
> Flounced petticoats with gowns divine,
>   O fie! ev'n *that's* not able.
>
> .   .   .   .   .

Thus while you warn a prince's ear
Of specious flattery to beware,
  You gild the gallic pill
In such a manner as to suit
Your honest views with George or Bute,
  And so farewell, dear Will.

His name, indeed, was public property. When
offensive allusions were to be made to Yorick it was
always masked under such shape as the " Reverend
Mr. S——e ;" but the Magdalen divine was named
openly and coarsely. A fiercer and more dangerous
pen than Scott's spoke of him boldly as

——that mild man of God,
The Reverend Doodle, Doctor Dodd.

And even in Goldsmith's last verses, in a corner of
that pleasant " Retaliation," full of delightful strokes,
comes an incidental hit, in which the Doctor's ill-re-
putation is assumed as a thing of course. Speaking
of Douglas, who had been " the scourge of impostors
and the terror of quacks," he bids all the " quacks,
bards, and quacking divines" dance with delight, for
they have nothing to fear now. And he goes on :
" Our Dodds shall be pious," &c. Churchill, too—
enemy to all shams, tearing off all masks, and with
the masks tearing away the skin, was not likely to
spare him, and in the terrible picture fitted into his
" Times," glances contemptuously at the fashionable
Dodd.

This was light treatment from so heavy a hand.
But five years after the Doctor had finished with
earthly intriguing, a bitter but truthful portrait of
the " Macaroni Parson" came from Cowper's pen ;
and from a single allusion to the diamond ring, there

can be no question but that he was sketching the
"unfortunate" Doctor. A more odious picture cannot be conceived:

> But loose in morals, and in manners vain,
> In conversation frivolous, *in dress*
> *Extreme, at once rapacious and profane,*
> Frequent in park with lady at his side,
> Ambling and prattling scandal as he goes:
> But rare at home, and never at his books,
> Or with his pen, save when he scrawls a card,
> Constant at routs, familiar with a round
> Of ladyships, a stranger to the poor,
> Ambitious of preferment for its gold.
>
> What! will a man play tricks—will he indulge
> A silly fond conceit of his fair form
> And just proportion, fashionable mien,
> And pretty face, in presence of his God?
> Or will he seek to dazzle one with tropes,
> As with the diamond in his City band?

With such a popular estimate of his character, it
seems indeed wonderful how he contrived to keep his
hold on the public. But he had "a party." He
had opened up new ground in the City—ground not
of such fine quality as he had hitherto worked, but
richer and more profitable. With the "City people"
he was the good man, preaching sweetly and tenderly,
delightful in company, active in charity, pleasant and
almost exciting to listen to at the Magdalen—and
therefore the butt of loose scoffers at the West-end.
And there was truth in this last view ; for, unluckily,
it was such men as Kenrick, and Parson Scott, and
Lord Sandwich, and March, and a hundred such, who
raised their voices and scoffed at the freedom of
the day.

.

CHAPTER THE SECOND.

A COURT SERMON.

IT was now come to the end of the year 1772, and this year brought with it an encouraging bit of preferment. He obtained the rectory of Hockliffe, in Bedfordshire, which was worth about one hundred and sixty pounds a year; and with this came, a little later, the vicarage of Chalgrove. The two together went a little in ease of the devouring annuities, and the "voluptuous" tavern dinners. But this preferment brought with it, also, an adventure which had near been fatal. He was coming up in his post-chaise with Mrs. Dodd from his new living, when he was stopped near the Tottenham-road turnpike by a mounted highwayman. This was the common probation for travellers making London; but this free-booter, who had some reputation in his profession, and was called William Griffith, turned back, as he was riding away, and discharged his pistol full at the window. The ball did no more damage than breaking the window: "happily, as it was *then thought,*" oddly adds "an editor" of one of the Doctor's books. Personal courage was said not to be one of his qualities; and in his evil day, when men with a strange lack of charity went about raking from corners, and sewers, and dust-bins, and publishing every degraded rumour and vulgar story that could be found, some one came with a legend of boyish London days, when he was in his teens. That he had attended a "Robin Hood" debating society, and that on one occasion, when a false alarm of fire had been given, he quite lost his wits, and was with difficulty restrained from dashing himself from the window. "This," says the person who reports the incident, "strikingly shows the *imbecility* of his character."

Doctor Dodd was, however, able to identify Mr. William Griffith, who, not long after, was taken and brought to trial. On December the 17th the Doctor appeared in the witness-box, and on his evidence the prisoner was found guilty. Twelve more were " capitally convicted" on the same day. A "long day" was allowed to the highwayman, and on the 20th of January, the following year, he went forth to execution, in one of the usual Monday morning dismal processions. "When the malefactors," says the reporter who attended, "stopped opposite to St. Sepulchre's to hear the dying words from the bellman, Bird" (one of Griffith's companions) "threw his face on the shoulders of the clergyman, and his form was agitated in a manner not to be described."

These horrible spectacles, reaching almost to barbarity, had affected Doctor Dodd very seriously, as indeed they had affected every good and thinking man in the kingdom. Such human sacrifices were a disgrace to the age, and a greater disgrace to the country—for it was truly stated at the time, that there was no other country in the world where such savage exhibitions were tolerated. Doctor Dodd, whose nature was all through amiable and philanthropic, put together a sermon on the subject; but, curious to say, it was in the very year that he had suffered from the attack of Griffith, and only a few months before the dismal procession, to which his evidence had contributed the highwayman, had stopped before St. Sepulchre's. This sermon was " On the Frequency of Capital Punishment ;" but in the introduction there is something very characteristic. " The following sermon," he says, " was intended to have been preached *in the Chapel Royal, St. James,* but was omitted *on account of the absence of the Court,* during the *author's month of waiting.*" Thus, everything he did was more or less to be marked with a little discoloration; and this flourish was only another instance of that weakness in every purpose of life, which was side by side with all his good intentions. He said justly that " it may seem strange, if not incredible, that of all the nations upon earth the laws of England are the most sanguinary; there being in them, as I am credibly informed, over a hundred and fifty capital cases." In a note he adds oddly, " See Ruffhead's Index to the Statutes." Then follows one of those curious passages in which he seems to anticipate his own crisis, and appears to plead pathetically for himself. If a civic crown was the reward of a Roman who saved a fellow-creature from death, what shall be his "who, by such a reformation, shall *save from an ignominious end* numbers of subjects and citizens, *hurried into eternity in the very bloom and flower of life, with all their sins and imperfections upon their heads, and cuts them off at once from all power of reformation, from all possibility of making amends to the state they have injured, to the friends they have alienated, and the God they have so daringly offended!*" This was, indeed, the substance of that bitter cry that was to come from his Newgate cell not half a dozen years later.

CHAPTER THE THIRD.

" DOCTOR SIMONY."

WITH this character, then, at the beginning of the year 1774, and with those who ministered to his pleasures pressing terribly and clamorously for food, he was at his wits' end for money. Suddenly, in January of that year, a Doctor Moss was advanced to the bishopric of Bath and Wells, and the rich and fashionable living of St. George's, Hanover-square, became vacant. Nothing could be more suited for one who was a fashionable preacher and, at the same time, embarrassed in his means. It was given out to be worth fifteen hundred pounds a year. It was not certain in whose gift was this prize—it being claimed by Lord North, the minister, by the Bishop of London, and by the Chancellor, Lord Apsley. It was assumed, however, as it eventually proved to be, that it was in the gift of the latter.

One day the Chancellor's wife, Lady Apsley, received a letter without a signature, asking her to exert her influence about this living, and offering her three thousand pounds down, with an annuity of five hundred pounds a year, if she would procure it for a person to be named later. She showed it to the Chancellor, who, thinking it a more serious affair than either she or the writer imagined it to be, set diligent inquiries on foot. It must have been clumsily done, for it was easily traced to a common law-clerk, and from the common law-clerk to Mrs. Dodd, the verger's daughter, and wife of the Reverend William Dodd, LL.D., one of his Majesty's chaplains. Mrs. Dodd, the law-clerk said, had dictated the whole to him. And Doctor Dodd, it was assumed, had inspired Mrs. Dodd.

At first the Doctor denied it boldly, and said he was not privy to the "officious zeal of his consort." When he found the Chancellor was in earnest, he begged delay, and offered to go abroad. Lord Apsley, however, went to the king, and laid the whole matter before him, who indignantly ordered his chamberlain to strike the offender's name from the list of his chaplains. Then the scandal became public. The news flew from coffee-house to coffee-house. When Lord Hertford told him of what he had been ordered to do, he complained bitterly of the cruelty with which he had been treated, and . once more denied the whole charge. In truth, his best excuse was the rude mechanism of the trick; and only for the fatal evidence of previous indiscretions, he might have successfully—had he chosen to brazen out his denial—tided over the accusation. But the public feeling became so angry and noisy

against him, that he actually addressed a weak,
piteous letter to the public journals, begging for
indulgence. It was dated on Feb. 10, 1774, and ran
thus:

" Sir,—May I earnestly entreat, through the chan-
nel of your paper, that the candid public will suspend
their sentence in my case? Under the pressure of
circumstances exceedingly adverse, and furnished with
no proofs of innocence but which are of a negative nature, there is left for me at present no mode of
defence, but that of an appeal to a life passed in the
public service, and an irreproachable attention to the
duties of my function. How impossible it is to oppose
the torrent of popular invective the world will judge.
It is hoped, however, that time will, ere long, put
some circumstances in my power which may lead to
an elucidation of this affair, convince to the satisfaction of mankind my integrity, and remove every ill
impression with regard to the proceedings which have
justly incensed a most respectable personage, and
drawn such misfortunes upon me.
                              " William Dodd."

Strange to say, he succeeded in dividing the town.
One half took his side. The congregations of the
Charlotte Chapels were a good constituency. The
City people held to him; and, stranger still, the
Methodists, whose enemy he was said to be, but whose
style he mimicked, were coming round to his party.
But for the present the current was too strong for
him, and he thought it prudent to retire abroad, and
hide his head for a while.

But when he was away he was to suffer a heavy
penalty for his offence. Foote was then pouring
forth that stream of farces which are perfect mirrors
for the manners of the day, and to which he gave a
vitality and vigour, by importing a rough coarse satire
on all prevailing weaknesses and follies. He dashed
these sketches in boldly, and with much force and
personality; and being at work on "The Cozeners,"
introduced a "Doctor Simony" and a "Mrs. Simony,"
whom there was no mistaking. It has been said
always, and repeated pretty often, that in this piece
Doctor Dodd was introduced upon the stage, but this
was not so. He is merely spoken of; and it is Mrs.
Simony—put for unhappy Mrs. Dodd—that was
brought before the audience. Mrs. Fleec'em, an intriguing lady, negotiates such delicate matters as the
procuring of places, at her house of business. Mrs.
Simony, Doctor Dodd's lady, comes to pay her a visit,
fresh from "Cox's Museum," where Sir Anthony
Absolute saw the automaton bull whose eye "rolled"
so terribly. "The Doctor knows nothing about it,"
she says, and then gives a sort of portrait which the
pit knew and roared at.

"The Doctor's powers are pretty well known about
town; not a more popular preacher within the sound
of Bow Bells; I do not mean for the mobility only—
these every canting fellow can catch; the best people
of fashion arn't ashamed to follow my Doctor. Not
one, madam, of the hundred drawling, long-winded
tribe; he never crams congregations, or gives them
more than they can carry away—not more than ten
or twelve minutes at most. . . . Even the Duchess

Dowager of Drowsy was never known to nod at my Doctor; and then he doesn't pore with his eyes close to the book like a clerk that reads the first lesson; not he, but all extemporary, madam; *with a cambric handkerchief in one hand and a diamond ring on the other; and then he waves this way and that way, and he courtsies, and he bows, and he bounces,* that all the people are ready to—— But then his wig, madam! I am sure you must admire his dear wig; not with the bushy brown buckles hanging and dropping like a Newfoundland spaniel, but short, *rounded off at the ear* to show *his plump cherry cheeks,* white as a curd, feather-topped, and the curls as close as a cauliflower.

"*Mrs. F.*—Why really, madam——

"*Mrs. Simony.*—Then my Doctor is none of your schismatics, madam: believes in the whole thirty-nine, and so he would if there were nine times as many.* . . . Not a step, I beseech you. Lord bless me! I had like to have forgot. . . . Besides all I have said, my Doctor, madam, possesses a *very pretty little poetical vein.* I have brought you here a little hymn in my pocket.†

"*Mrs. F.*—Hymn! Then the Doctor sings, I presume.

"*Mrs. Simony.*—Not a better pipe at the playhouse; he has been long notorious for that: then he is as cheerful, and has such a choice collection of songs; why he is constantly *asked to the great City feasts,* and does, I verily believe, more in-door christening than any three of the cloth."

* Here is the origin of Theodore Hook's old joke.
† An allusion to the Doctor's selection of Hymns for the Magdalen.

This is gay and very amusing; but, after all, it was an unwarrantable freedom. Doctor Dodd was fair game; but it was unmanly, gibbeting the poor foolish lady, whom even the law of that day would have assumed to have acted under her husband's influence. She was no more than a mechanical agent. But Foote only cared to find grist for his satirical mill, no matter where he had to look for it. It was a profitable and successful game, thus introducing notorious persons to excite the laughter of the pit, and he carried on his trade even at the sacrifice of the common feelings of gratitude and delicacy. A long list might be made of the persons whom this clever but cowardly mimic tried to hold up in his Shows, to earn money and popularity. A more odious calling cannot be conceived, or a more dangerous public nuisance. He was treated hospitably in Dublin, and received an uproarious welcome; but when he got back to London, sneered at the lieges who had welcomed him. The pleasant but eccentric Doctor Kennedy, friend of Sterne and Garrick, and of Foote's also, had a narrow escape of this pillory.* So, too, had a friend of Governor Thicknesse, whom he saved from this sort of exposure on a public stage. But the Welsh Mr. Ap-Rice, and Prince Boothby, and George Faulkner and his lameness, these were the men, some of whom were "friends," whom he ventured thus to turn to purposes of the vilest profit. Johnson he was burning to "take off" also, but that sturdy moralist asked his bookseller to send out for a thick cudgel—a sort of remonstrance

* Angelo's Memoirs.

which soon drifted to the professional satirist's ears,
and changed his purpose. Women were not likely
to send out for cudgels. But it is curious to think
that another such coarse attack upon another woman,
who had been similarly unfortunate, was his ruin.
His onslaught on the Duchess of Kingston destroyed
him.

Long after, when Dodd was lying in his prison,
this exposure came back to his mind. How deeply it
affected him may be seen in these bitter lines, which
form part of the retrospect of his entire life:

> Yes, yes, thou coward mimic, pampered vice,
> High praise be sure is thine. Thou hast obtained
> A worthy triumph. Thou hast pierced to the quick
> A weak, an amiable female heart—
> A conjugal heart most faithful, most attached;
> Yet can I pardon thee; for, poor buffoon,
> Thy vices must be fed; and thou must live,
> Luxurious live, a foe to God and man;
> Commissioned live, thy poison to diffuse,
> And taint the public virtue with thy crimes.
> Yes, I can pardon thee—low as thou art,
> And far too mean an object e'en of scorn.

It is in this transaction that the Doctor's conduct
stands out most unworthily. There was something
singularly shabby and unmanly—and even foolish, for
the device was transparent—in thrusting forward his
poor wife to public odium as the author of the act.
So much so, indeed, that the indignant lines he made
on Foote might apply with excellent force and appro-
priateness to himself.

Doctor Dodd, going abroad went straight to
Geneva, where his old pupil and constant patron was
staying. The new earl's patronage was not disturbed

by the late escapade. He either disbelieved it, or,
what is more probable, was careless whether it was true
or no. He must have been almost attached to him,
or have had that sort of tendency to his company
which men of pleasure have for each other's society,
and which stands in the room of affection; for we
have it on good Walpolean authority that the noble
pupil actually rode out several miles to meet the ar-
riving Doctor in some severe icy weather—so severe
that the pupil was frostbitten, and was laid up for a
long time after. In those times Geneva was very
far away, and we cannot tell how the story got
twisted, in travelling home to the clubs and coffee-
houses, and from them to Arlington-street. The
noble pupil treated him with great distinction, gave a
round of dinners in his honour, introduced him to
English and French, resident as well as vagabond,
and made much of him in a fashion that should have
been a warranty against the character in which he
was later to appear. Nay, he even presented him to
the living of Winge, in Buckinghamshire, so that
really he was almost encumbered with preferment.

Parting from this useful patron, he set off home by
way of Paris. There it was likely, that with his weak,
foolish, unballasted disposition, he should be shipwrecked. What a place Paris was then, what a vortex
of pleasure, Mercier tells us in his wonderful "Tableau
de Paris"—on the tone and details of which marvellous phantasmagoria it has not been noticed how much
Mr. Carlyle has modelled his French Revolution. So
strange and vivid a bird's-eye view of a city has never
yet been taken. Our Doctor was drawn into the gay

whirl. He left his gown and bands at his hotel, and
some one, who had gone out to the Plains of Sablons
to see the racing, one of the newest shapes of Anglo-
mania, brought back word to London how, to his
amazement, he had recognised the Magdalen preacher
in a carriage at the show, dressed in a mousquetaire
uniform—in very doubtful company—and gambling
away his money among the most eager of the French
roués.

CHAPTER THE FOURTH.

DOWNWARDS.

WHEN the scandal had blown over, and Dr. Simony was a little forgotten, he came home to England again. The state of London society at this date has been dwelt on before—its shameful toleration, and utter absence of moral purpose; so that it is no surprise to find our Doctor gradually gliding back again into his old pious groove. To show how little his disgrace had affected his position, a Mr. Hicks, about this time, sent in to the institution a full-length portrait of the Doctor, which was placed in the Board-room. But the following month, by a strange neglect, he absented himself for five Sundays, which was most probably the season he was exhibiting on the Plains of Sablons, and was "desired" in future to give "proper notice" if he could not come, and also not to absent himself, "except on account of ill health."*

With some, he was an impostor; but with the far

* MS. Registers.

greater number he had been persecuted for justice'
sake. So his popularity had scarcely diminished;
and by new exertions in a sort of philanthropic and
charitable direction, he brought over many more to
his side. He is said to have founded a Discharged
Prisoners' Aid Society, which is now flourishing and
full of vitality, in spite of the unsound touch that
helped to raise it up into life. He was a godly
man still with the crowd. "I do my best," writes one
Hoadly Ashe, who may be accepted as a fair type of
these admirers, "*and even the great Doctor Dodd* can
do do more. Oh, for his pen, and his melodious
voice! Pray give my respectful compliments to him."

This popular impression he kept alive and improved
by other means. All through his life he had a kind
of craze or fancy for devising Charities—and charities
of all kinds and degrees. It would almost seem as
though he had chosen this as a device for attracting
the notice of the town, and made it a useful instrument to acquiring the title of the "Great Doctor
Dodd." He could not have found time for more than
one or two of these charities; yet at his death he had
a whole sheaf of schemes ready for public introduction. In prison he made out a sort of blank verse cata-
logue of these labours, and poetically claimed credit
for all he had done. Among them was a Society for
the Release of Debtors; a charity for the Loan of
Money without Interest to Industrious Tradesmen,
the plan of which he had got from Dublin; and an
odd plan for "a National Female Seminary," which
had "received the approbation of some *very distinguished names*." This scheme would, no doubt, have

furnished some merriment to the free wits of the time.
But with the good works were other works. The old
extravagance, and the devouring annuities that fat-
tened on the extravagance, were strong as ever.
About this date we get a glimpse of him characteristic enough, meeting him, as it were, in the fashionable Parks.

That odd Governor Thicknesse—before alluded to
—who was essentially the man of a grievance, and
who had the knack all through life of stumbling from
one grievance to another, had for his arch-grievance
of all a quarrel with a Colonel Vernon. It seems as
though he had been harshly treated on the whole.
By-and-by Colonel Vernon bloomed into Lord Orwell,
grew old, as did Mr. Thicknesse; and finally, medi-
tating a tour to the south of France for his health,
received, on the eve of starting, a letter from his enemy.
It was to the effect, that as the peer was going to
France for his health, and Mr. Thicknesse for his purse
—also sadly out of sorts—they might both contrive to
meet " *and settle the little matter so long pending* between them." Of this significant proposal no direct
notice was then taken. But next day Mr. Thicknesse was wandering about the Park, when he fell in
with the gay Doctor Dodd, also taking the air. The
Doctor told him that only the day before he had been
dining with Lord Orwell, and (we now hear the
Doctor speaking for the first time) that the receipt
of the letter had been mentioned. " I have seen it,"
said Doctor Dodd, " and though I cannot justify his
conduct to you, still I think it was cruel towards him.
I do not think he will live six months. You have

hindered his southern expedition. He will not go, lest you should follow him. I, who have often attended such *high-crested* men upon their death-beds, could understand his real condition." Mr. Thicknesse parted from the Doctor, but was so affected by this picture, that he went straight to a coffee-house, and wrote a letter to Lord Orwell of quite another tone and pattern—possibly as the Doctor intended he should do. For it requires little penetration to see that the smooth Doctor was sent, as an envoy, to skilfully soothe down the troublesome fellow who had a grievance, and arrange for his lordship's quiet travelling. So was that other Doctor accredited by Selwyn to arrange *his* unpleasant business. With this squares wonderfully a story whispered by Walpole—a torn rag of gossip—which deals, also, with an embassy. The noble pupil, whose chaplain he was, required some return for his favours; and, anxious to make some sort of reparation to a young person whom he had injured, sent his chaplain as his ambassador, with no less a sum than one thousand pounds. Such a trait was not very common in the fine gentlemen of the day, who were as cruel as they were fine. But it was said—with what truth we know not, but it is to be feared with some probability—that the reverend envoy kept back nine hundred pounds of the sum for his own devouring emergencies! If it be true, it was a far more capital offence than the one for which he suffered.*

But now his unsteadiness was affecting his position

---

* See later, Toplady's letter exhorting him to make reparation for something that seems to have very much the same character.

in life seriously. The last committee that he attended
at the Magdalen was in January, 1773. In August
of the following year another chaplain was appointed
in his room. The directors' patience was, no doubt,
worn out.* He was sinking deeper and deeper in
the mire of embarrassment. "He descended *so
low*," says the servants'-hall style of memoir before
alluded to, "*as to become the editor of a newspaper.*"
What the fatal journal was which had become the
instrument of his abasement, has not been discovered.
A more certain token of his embarrassment is, that
there was a rumour abroad of his trying to have himself
discharged from his debts by a commission in bank-
ruptcy, but failed. He was hurrying on fast to the
end, with scarcely time to look before or behind him
—precipitated forward by his furies of debt and difficulty—and literally did not know where to turn to.
Characteristically appealing to clap-trap sympathies,
he now thought of the Freemasons, and was busy
with a history of that order when the catastrophe
came.

* MS. Registers of the Magdalen.

CHAPTER THE FIFTH.

TOWN TALK.

IT was now come to the year 1776. Early in that year we hear him appealing from the pulpit in the "Anniversary Sermon of the Society for the Recovery of Drowned Persons," at St. Anne's, to "a very numerous congregation." His exertions for that society were to aid him later in a way that he little dreamed of. We hear him, too, from a less becoming stage, making an "Oration at Freemasons' Hall," with what aim or purpose we know not. Finally, on February the 24th of that year, he disposed of his Pimlico chapel, and Doctor Courtenay, of St. George's, Hanover-square—a name which could not have rung pleasantly in his ears—succeeded him. Our Doctor, however, retained a little interest in the chapel, and "by purchase," says the account, "acquired a fourth part *of the concern.*" It was, no doubt, pecuniary pressure that forced him to this step; and, indeed, the luckless Doctor was now being hemmed into that fatal corner whence he was to strive to escape by a step yet more fatal.

He was still popular, and his sermons were always well attended. There must have been something attractive, and even "sensational," to use that hackneyed word, in a preacher who used to ascend the pulpit with a bouquet, and a diamond ring glittering on his finger, whose robes exhaled sweet perfumes, and the snowy white of whose hand was conspicuously displayed. These might have been idle West-end stories, but they got into print. The sermons themselves must have been welcome, even for their manner, which was in contrast to the cold sterility of the pulpit oratory of the day; for the Doctor used to get his by heart instead of reading them, and deliver them with much energy and dramatic effect. As a sarcastic critic remarked, there was "a general appositeness of his *genteel action* to his eloquent discourse." The admiration of an enraptured auditor found expression in the following lines:

ON HEARING DR. DODD PREACH.

Heard but the libertine thy pulpit lore,
Pathetic Dodd! the wretch would sin no more.
Touched with thy preaching, *dulness* waves his sleep,
And *levity* itself is seen to weep.
Let flattered greatness still by fools be sung;
With *Dodd's* applause what temples have not rung?
Go on, judicious pastor!—awe the bold,
And still improve the young, reclaim the old;
With pleasing energy the Saviour preach,
And virtue animate, and candour teach.

Still make fair chastity the darling theme;
Whilst Magdalens support and prize its fame.
Then—nor till late—may Heaven reward thy care,
And make thee *angel* in a brighter sphere!

In a pleasant *Town and Country Magazine* of the time, it was said, with a curious spirit of prophecy, that "gaiety and dissipation soon convinced him that he was pursuing a career that must terminate in his destruction." And actually in that year we find him held up for public tattle, if not for public scandal (for then the town was not to be scandalised by anything), framed in one of the well-known little *tête-à-tête* medallions, and joined with another of a Mrs. Robinson. True, he was merely set down as "The Macaronic Parson, Mr. D——," and the lady as Mrs. R——n; but there was no misunderstanding the allusion, rendered more plain by bringing in C—— Chapel.

If we are to accept this pasquinade as authentic, it would seem that about this date his extravagance had led him to the King's Bench Prison—or at least that such a belief was abroad. And there, it was said, that he made acquaintance with this Mrs. R——n, also in durance for a life of extravagance. "Compassion," we are told, "induced her first to extend her benevolence to our hero, who found her acquaintance very convenient and eligible about three o'clock, where he had always had a strong *penchant* for a good dinner." When he obtained his liberty, and recommenced his sermons, he found himself receiving several presents from an anonymous donor, whom he presently discovered to be Mrs. Robinson; and, in return, "sent her

some game, of which he was requested to partake."
This contemptible chit-chat, in the very lowest style
of scandal-mongering, is worthy of no notice here,
beyond this significance, that it shows with what freedom the idle tongues of the day dealt with his name.
They were presently to be yet more busy; for we
are now at the year 1777, when, for many weeks, the
whole kingdom shall do nothing but talk of Doctor
Dodd.

CHAPTER THE SIXTH.

THE FATAL BOND.

To his living in Bucks—one of his little benefices —he had paid but four flying visits, and had preached four times; and it was remarked afterwards by the inhabitants, who were seldom gratified by hearing the fashionable London preacher, what a strange significance there was in the texts he had chosen. When the story of his fate drifted down to them from London, the sermons, and the texts of the sermons, were recollected, and it was thought how they shadowed forth a glimpse of coming destiny. It did seem as though he had some such uneasy sense hanging over him, when he could choose such a theme as this:

"Rejoice not against me, O mine enemy. When I fall I shall arise!"

Or, upon another Sunday, a still more significant text:

"Thy life shall hang in doubt before thee, and thou shalt fear day and night, and shall have none assurance of thy life. In the morning thou shalt say,

H

Would God it were even ; and at even thou shalt say,
Would God it were morning!"

But all through his life some such mysterious sense
of a gloomy end seemed to oppress him.

It was now the beginning of the year, and Doctor
Dodd was being very hard pressed indeed. He had
moved to Argyle-street. He had been obliged to
part with his Bloomsbury chapel ; but in this transaction a rumour, not to his credit, had gone abroad.
To the two clergymen who were treating with him,
he represented the value of the " concern " at over
five hundred a year. It was found, after the bargain had been concluded, that it was scarcely worth
half that sum, and by the arrangement one of the
clergymen was said to have been ruined. The Doctor
owed rent which was heavily in arrear, and the furniture was already burdened with two bills of sale or
executions. Some heavy "tradesmen's bills" were
pressing him, and he literally knew not which side
to turn. Money *must* be had.

There was a Mr. Robertson in the City, a stockbroker, who procured moneys on discount, and on
Saturday, the 1st of February, he was surprised by a
visit from the well-known Doctor Dodd. The business that brought him was money. The tutorship
and patronage of Lord Chesterfield was matter of
notoriety in London—it was one of the secrets of the
reverence with which the Doctor was regarded ; and
that such a wealthy and influential friend should
assist his old tutor was to be expected. On this occasion the Doctor brought with him a bond, which
his noble pupil, the earl, had filled in, for four thou-

sand two hundred pounds, and on which he thought
some money could be raised. Nothing would be more
natural than that the tutor should apply for aid to
the pupil, or that the latter should supply it. It was
left with the broker, who undertook to negotiate the
affair. Sunday intervened, on which day the Doctor
preached with great pathos and effect. On Monday,
Mr. Franco, of Fenchurch-street, gave a large dinner-
party to the popular clergyman and others, and in
the evening the broker saw him there, and brought
the bond with him to report progress. A Mr. Fletcher
had been discovered in the City, who had agreed to
furnish the money on the terms of an annuity of
seven hundred pounds; a proper warrant of attorney
to confess judgment had been prepared, and all was,
in fact, happily arranged. The bond was left with the
Doctor for his patron's execution; and the next morning the broker attended in Argyle-street to complete
the business. The earl's signature had been obtained.
The intimacy of the two was so well known, that in
a pleasant, informal way the Doctor merely mentioned
that he had *seen* him sign, and would now attach his
own signature as witness. With the same friendly
irregularity the broker became another witness to the
earl's signature which he had *not* seen attached, and
took the Doctor's word that all was right. There was
another document—a receipt of the earl's for the
money; both were completed with all formality, and
the money was paid. There were still some scruples;
but the Doctor, to quiet them, came furnished with *a
letter from Lord Chesterfield*—a fact which in the
popular accounts of the case has never been men-

tioned. Next day the instruments were transferred to Mr. Manley, an intelligent London solicitor, who acted for Mr. Fletcher, the lender.

While looking through them, his attention was attracted by "a very remarkable blot," on the *e* in the word "seven" (part of the description—"four thousand seven hundred pounds"). There were scratches of a pen, too, above and below the blot. There was really nothing suspicious in this; for, as the solicitor frankly owned, he "could see no end it would answer." It was only part of the unlucky fatality that pursued the Doctor. It was so odd—possibly so unmeaning—that he thought he would see his principal, or, at least, have a clean, new bond made out. However, the result of seeing the principal was the more sensible course, which should have been thought of at first—of seeing the earl himself in person. The solicitor called on Thursday—then "took the liberty" of writing to say he would call again the following morning. He came at ten. Lord Chesterfield met him on the stairs, and said: "You have come about a bond? But I have paid it long ago, and burnt it," he added. This mystified the solicitor a good deal. It was then explained that the earl had given a bond for five hundred pounds when he was a minor, but when he was of full age he had destroyed it. He added, that the whole matter was secret. The solicitor, still more perplexed, told him he did not understand his meaning, and "introduced the bond in question to his lordship." Then all was explained. The signature was repudiated. The whole was a forgery—and a clever forgery—both the bond and the reassuring letter.

In the mean time the lender also was a little disturbed in his mind, and had that morning gone to
Robertson to say, that the annuity (seven hundred
pounds) seemed suspiciously large in proportion to
the sum it was to secure. The broker was quieting
his mind by saying that Lord Chesterfield was to
repay it in a year, when Manley entered fresh from
Lord Chesterfield with news of the discovery.

The next question was what was to be done. The
money had been paid; and the noble pupil had suggested that, most likely, the Doctor had gone off.
Assuming this to be the case, they went straight to
the lord mayor, at Guildhall, and obtained warrants
against both the broker and the clergyman—an unfortunate assumption, as well as unfortunate action,
founded upon that assumption. Had they gone to
look for Dodd first, the thing would never have gone
beyond a town scandal, and the Doctor might have
finished his life—disreputably—as a sort of loose
privateer parson, of which there were many then
upon the social high seas.

With two officers and the warrant, they went first
to secure Robertson, the broker, whom they found in
Sir Charles Raymond's banking-house. They then
set off for Argyle-street, for the Doctor. They were
shown into the parlour. The wretched man came
down to them all aghast, and asked their business.
The attorney told him he " was sorry to attend him
upon so unhappy occasion." (So public a character
was the Doctor, that every one seemed to be making
him apologies through every stage of the process.)
He was much struck, said the attorney, and remained

silent for some time. They then asked him what could have induced him to do such a thing. The Doctor, not attempting any denial, said, that it was urgent and terrible necessity—that he was forced to meet some tradesmen's bills—that he meant no injury to Lord Chesterfield, or to any one—that he meant to pay all back in six months—and that he had certain resources—with much more in the same piteous strain.

The solicitor then asked him if he had any of the money to restore, as that was the only possible means that could save him. He said that he had some of it; and desired to go up-stairs to fetch it. To this the officers demurred; and it was only on the solicitor going with him, and not letting him out of sight, that it was allowed. The Doctor went to his bureau, and, from a pigeon-hole in the bureau, took out six bills of five hundred pounds each, on Sir Charles Raymond's house. That made up three thousand of the four thousand two hundred pounds. He then got out his banker's book, by which he tried to show that some nine hundred pounds or so were to his credit there; and the solicitor said it seemed to be so. But he owned, previously, that he could not draw for more than five or six hundred of this sum. A cheque was then filled in on the Exchange Banking Company, in St. James's-street, for five hundred pounds (how the unhappy Doctor's pen must have quivered as he wrote); and then they came down stairs again to the parlour.

It must have been at this time that a strange chance of deliverance was purposely offered to him—for when they were at the bureau, Mr. Manley left him a moment alone. The bond was on the table, and a bright fire was burning in the grate. When Mr. Manley returned, the bond was there still. A foolish presumption of the Doctor's conscious innocence was afterwards based on this forbearance; but, those at all familiar with criminal cases, will set it down to ignorance, or the want of thought; or, perhaps, to the hesitation of a weak mind at so bold and dangerous a step. Certainly it was hard measure to keep the bond which had been all but discharged.

It was now between five and six o'clock. The Chevalier Ruspini had a dinner-party that day in Pall-Mall, at which the Doctor was to have been present. An apology was sent at once. The guests perhaps wondered was the agreeable Doctor ill, for he was not likely to deny himself a pleasant party.* But some one dropping in later in the evening, told the astonished company the reason of this absence, now all over the town.

Everything seemed to be done in great agitation. The broker, whose position was almost as critical, hurriedly drew a cheque on his own bankers for one hundred pounds—the commission he had received. That left just six hundred pounds to be accounted for. The only thing now was to see Lord Chesterfield—report to him this partial restitution—and hear his determination.

Meanwhile, the officers and the unhappy Doctor were to retire to the York Coffee-house, in St. James's-square, and await their return. After, no doubt, a sickening interval of suspense, the solicitor

* Taylor represents him as being arrested at Ruspini's; but the sworn testimony at the trial supports the views given.

appeared again with Fletcher the lender, and a Mr. Corry, Lord Chesterfield's confidential solicitor. A private room was ordered up-stairs, to which they all removed.

Doctor Dodd was then asked if he could give reasonable security for the balance? He answered, "Very readily;" that he was willing to give any in the world. It was proposed that he should execute a warrant of attorney to confess judgment upon his goods and furniture, which, though already under a distress and execution, were valuable enough to meet this claim also. This document was drawn out on the spot—attested by Corry and Manley. Then the Doctor said he thought he could draw for a couple of hundred more on his banker. "If you can," said the solicitor, "it will be much better;" and this reduced the judgment and security to some four hundred pounds only. Things, therefore, were in a fair way of being adjusted. There was hope for the wretched Doctor. The thing would be accommodated. It was too late that night to set him free from the officers; but to-morrow that could be arranged. Meanwhile, an agitating, fluttering day was over.

All seemed to have behaved with great consideration in this unhappy affair, and to have tried to help off Doctor Dodd in every way they could; and he went to bed that night relieved by the assurance that no further steps would be taken against him. But what now seems to have been a wretched fatality at this precise juncture, destroyed him.

CHAPTER THE SEVENTH.

COMMITTED TO "THE COMPTER."

THE next morning was Saturday morning. Lord Chesterfield came down to Mr. Fletcher, at the banking-house of Sir Charles Raymond; and a message was sent over to the lord mayor, then sitting, to know when he would be willing to receive them. The answer brought back was, that the prisoner was then actually before him. They hurried over. But the lord mayor had insisted on going into the case. Indeed, all parties seem to have been under some strange misapprehensions about the powers of magistrates and prosecutors, and to have forgotten that compounding a felony is a serious offence against British law. Once the process of law has been put in motion, it is almost impossible, or requires infinite skill and something like collusion in the authorities, to check it.

The name of this lord mayor was Halifax. It was said afterwards, that he had acted with violence —certainly with haste; and the excuse made for him was the natural impetuosity of his temper.* If

* Letter to Fletcher and Peach.

he had, indeed, hurried on the matter, and dealt too harshly with Dodd, there would be some excuse for Lord Chesterfield. But in the heat of public excitement these charges were shifted on to every party in the affair in turn, and it was the sheerest ignorance and absurdity to expect that the chief magistrate of a great city could compound a charge of this nature in open court, especially in the case of so public and well-known a character as Doctor Dodd.

The charge was entered on; both Mr. Manley and Lord Chesterfield had to give their evidence; and both were bound over to prosecute. This must have come like a thunderbolt on the wretched prisoner, who had considered his escape all but secure; and he made an agitated, incoherent protest to the magistrate.

"I cannot tell what to say in such a situation; I had no intention to defraud Lord Chesterfield. I hope his lordship will consider my case. . . . I meant it as a temporary resource. I have made satisfaction, and I hope it will be considered. I was pressed exceedingly for some three hundred pounds to pay some bills due to tradesmen. I should have repaid it in half a year. My Lord Chesterfield cannot but have some tenderness for me, as my pupil. I love him." (Here his tears interrupted him.) "He knows I revere his honour as dear as my honour. I hope he will accord to me that mercy that is in his heart, and show clemency to me. There is nobody wishes to prosecute. Pray, my lord mayor, consider this, and discharge me."

There is something wild and very piteous in this

appeal. It *could* bring no fruit, as Mr. Manley could have told him. His friends were powerless—mere instruments in the hands of the law.

Robertson, who was a young man, and who, it was said, behaved with the consciousness of innocence, then called out : "I hope, Doctor, you will do me the justice to declare publicly that I am nowise guilty."

The prisoner answered, "I do! I do! I do!"

Fletcher, the defrauded banker, it was noticed, now showed no eagerness to prosecute, having got back nearly all his money. But though Manley insisted strongly that Lord Chesterfield should be the prosecutor, the lord mayor eventually bound over Fletcher and Peach—as indeed was only legal and proper—in a penalty of five hundred pounds. Thus the distressing scene ended. The Doctor was led away to Wood-street Compter on foot, which gave the mob an opportunity of jeering at him, and of adding to his miseries. No wonder that when he reached his prison the wretched Doctor fainted away several times. And on that Saturday morning, the well-known Doctor Dodd, the fashionable preacher, was committed to take his trial. All London read it in their evening paper, and there was no sermon in Bedford-street that night.

The conduct of Lord Chesterfield all through this transaction seems, at first sight, to bear out the popular prejudice associated with his name. When it is considered that no practical injury was done to him beyond the freedom taken with his name, and when, besides, a question arose as to taking Lord Chesterfield's testimony on his oath or on " his honour," he almost in-

sisted on being sworn, to avoid all fear of irregularity
—putting these things together with the sort of promise
given the night before, the pupil's behaviour might
seem harsh and cruel. The odious celebrity which he
for long after enjoyed of "having hung a parson," was
thought to have some just foundation. The reasonable
explanation seems to be, that he was young, and in the
hands of legal advisers who thought impunity for so
enormous a sum would be a dangerous precedent, and
encourage others to victimise a young nobleman. Perhaps, too, he really resented the effrontery of the deed,
and the scandal of the transaction ; or perhaps—which
may be the true reason—he had no real feeling towards
his old tutor, and their friendship only bore the
rotten fruit which all convivial friendships are sure to
bear.

The fact is, his share in the matter was purely
negative. His influence might have done something,
and this he did not exert. Manley, Fletcher's solicitor,
was the active mover in the business from beginning
to end, even to the illegal procuring an order to bring
up witnesses at Hicks's Hall. It was said at the
time that the money-lenders were furious at having
lost a bargain that was almost usurious in its character, being "three times the interest allowed by law,"
and that there was a suspicious eagerness about the
transaction.* Lord Chesterfield's known wealth and
position should have told them that he was "likely
to be his own banker," and unlikely to employ his
tutor to raise money for him. Further, to make the
transaction more profitable, the bills were not payable

* Letter to Fletcher and Peach.

until fourteen days after date, and no interest was allowed for that time.* On the whole, therefore, we may fairly acquit the pupil of any important share in his tutor's ruin. Still, making every allowance for his position, there are facts at this stage of the case which show that he was more eager in the prosecution than he need have been; for it was remarked, when the noble pupil came forward, the unhappy Doctor made all sorts of signs and piteous appeals to come near and speak to him, of which Lord Chesterfield took not the least notice. The state of the unhappy clergyman at this stage was pitiable indeed. He was almost beside himself, and could hardly articulate. For he must have considered his escape all but certain, and it did appear that some sort of engagement had been entered into the evening before.

That night the story was all over London. The whole town had the details. Doubting friends and scoffing enemies said now that what they had anticipated had come to pass. We may get a faint conception of the tone of the public by imagining ourselves to hear some night of the arrest and committal for some crime of some popular preacher who had been for years a town attraction.

Outside, in the streets, the story was told and sung. The refined Doctor and his offence came to the mouths of the low ballad-singers. This shape of degradation must have been carried out to a greater extent than usual; for Johnson, in one of his written pleas for the Doctor, takes notice of it. The life of a ballad is rarely longer than a single day; but one of

* Letter to Fletcher and Peach.

these broadsides, sung in the streets on this evening,
has been preserved, and may still be seen—printed on
the true coarse paper, and headed by a vile cut of a
figure with three heads, half of whose body is dressed
like a clergyman, the other half like a beau.* It ran :

A NEW SONG.

Dear reverend sirs, if on you I may call,
The advice that you give us is nothing at all ;
Tho' to you these few lines may appear somewhat odd,
Only think of the case now of good Doctor Dodd.

Who'd think that the shepherd should lead us astray,
When thumping the cushion and loudly would sway,
And tell us so gravely we all must fear God,
But the Devil I fear will have good Doctor Dodd.

The lambs of the Magdalen good he would teach,
And turn up his eyes and against sin would preach,
If he'd see you but smile, why he'd give you a nod,
The sanctified reverend good Doctor Dodd.

But money, poor soul, led the Doctor astray,
Four thousand two hundred!   Good Lord, let us pray
That the Doctor himself may receive his reward,
And Jack Ketch, poor soul, tuck him up in a cord.

When before my Lord Mayor his defence he did make,
The tears flowed so fast he hardly could speak :
Let mercy rule justice, in that you'll serve God,
So great was the prayers of the good Doctor Dodd.

Robertson the broker here made his defence.
" Do me justice, good Doctor, prove my innocence."
" I do! I do! I do!"—then heaving a sob,
So penitent, truly, is good Doctor Dodd.

But for trial, alas! the good Doctor is sent,
For forgery a halter must be the event ;
For a time there we'll leave him to feast on salt cod—
May all rogues have their due, so I wish Doctor Dodd.

* See the curious Roxburgh Collection of Ballads in the British
Museum.

Another of these ballads has been preserved, and in this fashion was the unfortunate man hoarsely sung:

Come let us all pray for protection
  To our gracious Heavenly God,
Lest we have cause for deep reflection,
  Like the unhappy Doctor Dodd;
Who though so great, so fine a preacher,
  And once a chaplain, as they tell,
This reverend and learned teacher,
  How alas, alas! he fell.

He forged the bond, it was purporting
  To be the bond of a noble peer,
Four thousand two hundred pounds it mentions,
  Which Doctor Dodd received were clear.
He paid the broker he employed
  For his trouble, without doubt;
And in a very few days after,
  This forgery it was found out.

His yearly income, we are informed,
  Was five or six hundred so round,
And if he could not live upon it,
  How must a' curate with forty pound?
But pride and luxury bring ruin,
  And to the greatest misery,
Now this was Doctor Dodd's undoing,
  And set him upon forgery.

On the 19th of February the Bench of Aldermen had been applied to, to make an order to bring up Robertson from Newgate, that his evidence might be taken. But the City magistrates refused to grant it. Later, however, Manley's clerk came again, and secretly prevailed on Deacon, who was Clerk of the Arraigns, to give him such an order. On which Robertson was brought up and examined before the grand jury. By this unworthy artifice important evidence was secured. But when the news reached his City friends on the bench, the Old Bailey was thrown into confusion. The aldermen were indignant, and the clerk was severely reprimanded. It was to prove, however, a fortunate mistake for the Doctor, and furnished him with some more weeks of life.

Indeed, all through, he was treated with the greatest consideration, and rules were stretched unwarrantably in his favour. He had friends in the Lord Mayor's Court among the aldermen, who interfered, and had the order cancelled. Much confusion and argument was brought about by this step; and one of the judges, at the trial, alluded in strong language to, what he called, the "improper lenity" that had been shown the prisoner, in putting him on a different footing from his fellows. For it seems that, with a view of sparing him, he had not been brought up six days before the sessions, as the ordinary accused had been.

The grand jury found the bills, at Hicks's Hall, "before me," says Sir John Hawkins, with great complacency.

On the 1st of March was to be read in the papers, "A Card," unmistakably his composition, and in which, with his old bad taste and indiscretion, he tries to appeal from the tribunal that had just dealt with him. He offered thanks to all the sympathisers who had thought of him in his distress; regretted that business had hitherto prevented his receiving "the favour of their proffered visits" at Wood-street, but that *now* he would be at any time happy to receive their friendly and Christian consolation. This was, in fact, a wholesale invitation to the town, and looks like a skilful attempt to widen the field of sympathy by direct personal intercourse. And, as it proved, there were numbers of utter strangers who were eager to avail themselves of the opportunity. "Perfectly at ease," the "Card" went on, "with respect to his fate, and thoroughly resigned to the will of God, he cannot but feel *a complacency* in the striking humanity which he has experienced. And while he most earnestly entreats a continuance and increase of that spirit of prayer which he is told is poured forth for him, he cannot omit to assure all who have expressed their sympathy for him, that, *conscious of the purity of his intention* from any purpose to do injury, and relying on the full proof of that *intention*, by having done no injury to any man, in respect to this unfortunate prosecution, he fully reposes himself on the goodness of his God," &c. In short, his weak, quibbling subterfuge about the "intention to defraud," which even poor as a plea at the bar of the court, became contemptible in a serious appeal to the country.

The "Card" was followed up by an indiscreet attempt of the same class to raise sympathy; and in every newspaper were to be read, "Verses by an unhappy Prisoner," to this halting chant:

> Amid confinement's miserable gloom,
> Midst the lone horrors of this miserable room, &c.

No wonder that the tone and spirit of these claptraps were commented on hostilely, it being "highly derogatory to the honour of the Almighty to make him out a peculiar favourer of criminals." And the Doctor was then reminded of some home truths

very much to the point. Had he thought that what
he had done was forgery, which was only another
shape of a lie—had he thought of the bad example
and scandal—had he thought of the injury he was
doing to a young nobleman just entering on life,
when a bond to such an amount would be going
round the market—had he thought of the irreparable
injury done to the innocent stockbroker whom he
had brought to a gaol? This was plain speaking; but
still fair criticism on the Doctor's sickly appeals.

A week after, at the Magdalen Chapel, the clergyman who was officiating in the chaplain's absence
read out a paper which he said had been sent to him:
"The prayers of this congregation are desired for an
unhappy person in confinement, and under very great
affliction of mind." If the tears of the Magdalen
had been so ready in the latticed gallery at the
Doctor's sermons, how they must have flowed at this
significant notice. But he did not know at this time
what the town knew—that his picture, which hung
in all state in the Board-room of the Magdalen House,
had been ignominiously taken down, and carried away
to some private place—the governors, no doubt,
finding it awkward to have the "great Doctor Dodd"
looking down on them as they deliberated.*

---

* *Lady's Magazine,* 1777. Was this the fine portrait of the Doctor
by Gainsborough?

CHAPTER THE EIGHTH.

" THE TRIAL."

SATURDAY, the 2nd of February, came round, and Doctor Dodd was placed at the bar. The morning of the sessions arrived, and the real moment of the Doctor's exposure was to begin. There were crowds gathered to see the show—just as crowds had so often before gathered to see and hear him at the Magdalen. This dreadful ordeal he had now to pass through. He appeared in the dock supported by his friend Weedon Butler. The judges who were to try him were, Mr. Justice Willes, Mr. Justice Peryn, and Mr. Justice Gould. For the Crown appeared Mr. Mansfield and Mr. Davenport. For the prisoner, Cowper, Buller, and Howarth ; of whom the two first were to be judges later. The popular preacher was not likely to want the best assistance that money could procure. They must have felt, however, that it was a desperate case, and they could rely but on the feelings of the jury, and on a pre-

I 2

liminary objection. When the prisoner was being indicted, he begged leave to read a paper, and the severity of those days not allowing the accused the benefit of a speech from his counsel, and even forcing him to open matter of legal objection, Doctor Dodd proceeded to say, that as Robertson's name was on the back of the bill found by the grand jury, and as *that* testimony had been placed before them by surreptitious means, and in defiance of the order of the court, he was advised the indictment could not be sustained; and thereupon his counsel proceeded to argue the legal question.

It was, what might be called, a "nice point," and on account of the greater indulgence extended to prisoners in the construction of criminal doubts, might seem to offer a fair chance; and a very spirited argument followed. It was evident that the counsel for the defence strained every nerve to carry this point. Lord Hale, and many other authorities, were quoted; and it did seem founded in justice that the prisoner should not be affected by a witness who was himself open to the same charge, and whose evidence, as it was illegally obtained, should practically be assumed not to have been before the grand jury. Mr. Mansfield, on the other side, in a calm and logical argument, disposed of the objection; declared that it was "perfectly new" to him; that it was no concern of the court what evidence was before the grand jury, or how it came to them; neither were they to weigh its legality or illegality; but it was quite sufficient that the bill was found.

It was then urged as good law, that where the

bill had been found on the testimony of an outlaw the indictment had been quashed. The Crown replied that Robertson was not to be considered a criminal, as was the outlaw. Here, however, he was stopped by the court, who said they had it in the commitment before them, that Robertson was described as a principal. They offered the Crown to let them prefer a new indictment, or else go on with the present one at their peril, and have " the point saved" for the opinion of the judges. By this latter course, even if the prisoner was found guilty, and the judges decided with him, he never could be indicted on the same charge again—so there was a good deal of risk in adopting it; but so confident were the Crown in this view of the law, that they elected to take the chance.

It has been mentioned how he had managed to attach the " City people" to him. It was not therefore surprising, that, after the argument had closed, Alderman Woolridge stood up, and in a warm and excited speech, in which we almost hear his voice trembling, spoke of the proceeding as "an order wickedly, fraudulently, and maliciously obtained," and perhaps by something worse than all these epithets. " It strikes me with astonishment," the alderman went on; " I know nothing of the law; I speak from what I feel in my own heart. I say, if the prisoner at the bar is convicted by means of this order being surreptitiously obtained, *I would not stand in the clerk's place for all it is worth! I say, let him hold up his hand and say whether he does not think the blood of the man at the bar will fall upon his head!*"

This strange burst signifies something more than mere displeasure at an irregularity in the court, and shows how excited men's minds were about the unhappy Doctor's case. No notice was taken of these remarks, and the trial went on.

The Doctor was accordingly indicted in eight counts, framed with the usual ingenious variations, so as to cover all the degrees of delinquency into which the offence could be tortured. Mansfield stated the case in a calm and temperate discourse, opening his speech with an allusion to the extraordinary degree it had been a subject of conversation for the past fortnight, and exhorting the jury to dismiss all rumours from their minds. Witnesses were then called, whose testimony, dovetailed together, make up the story of the fraud just given. There were some singular violations of the law of evidence tolerated by the judges. For instance, the whole of the Doctor's behaviour, speeches, and confession, and admissions, on and after his arrest, when *no caution* had been given to him, were received. So, too, Mr. Manley, the solicitor, was allowed to tell all that passed between him and Lord Chesterfield when he called on him—together with the earl's remarks and denial of the bond. And when this was faintly and doubtingly objected to by the prisoner's counsel, the judge remarked, " Surely we have only to ask Lord Chesterfield himself," as though it was to save time.

Presently the earl was placed in the witness-box, amid great sensation in the court, for the relation

between the pupil and patron was well known, and
to the great agitation of the prisoner in the dock.
" O, that eternal night," he wrote from his cell,
" had in that moment screened me from myself, My
Stanhope to behold !"

But that evidence was decisive. Everything was
only too clear. The case for the prosecution closed,
and then Mr. Justice Peryn said, " Now, Doctor
Dodd, this is the time for you to make your defence
to what the witnesses have said." And Doctor Dodd
then spoke his defence—a very pathetic and moving
address, but which was yet, after all, no defence. He
said he was advised that the Act of Parliament " runs
perpetually in that style—*with an intention* to *defraud*," but that in his mind there could have been
none such, for he had restored and meant to restore
what he had taken.* He had made a perfect and

---

* The Act under which the prisoner was indicted was one passed in
the year 1729, which made the punishment capital, in consequence of
the increase of the " pernicious and *abominable* crimes" of perjury and
forgery. Up to the year 1821 the succession of victims had been kept
up steadily, when the punishment was commuted to transportation,
with some exceptions, and notably that of forging a will. And the
first year of the present reign was happily inaugurated by a complete
abrogation of capital punishment for such offences. The Act of
George the Second runs exactly as the Doctor pleaded, " with an intention to defraud ;" and it shows that his advisers must have been at
their wits' end for an excuse, when they had nothing better to suggest.
The law has no means of ascertaining the secret *intentions* of delin-
quents ; it can only deal with their acts. For every criminal act
the law supplies a criminal intention; and it lies on the prisoner to
remove this presumption by proof. Here the offence was *complete*,
and the Doctor's intention to restore the money—if it really existed
—would have been merely a sort of atonement, which in our own day

ample restitution. "I leave it, my lords, to you, and gentlemen of the jury, to consider, if an unhappy man does transgress, what can God and man desire more?" He then added, that he had been "pursued with the most oppressive cruelty, prosecuted after the most express engagement, after the most delusive and *soothing arguments*" (a curious expression) "from Mr. Manley." Death, he owned, would be the most pleasant of all blessings after this place. But he would be glad to live for the sake of his wife, who, for twenty-seven years, had been "an unparalleled example of conjugal affection to me, and whose behaviour in this crisis would draw *tears of approbation* from the most inhuman." He then urged that his creditors would suffer cruelly by his death. All of which were idle topics, and could have no effect with men who consider their oath, and the stern duty cast upon them by that oath. So, indeed, the judge hinted, who owned that this had been "a very pathetic address." But he could scarcely pass by the weakness of the Doctor's defence. As to his having no intention to defraud, and a purpose to

might have been considered in passing sentence. A few weeks later, in that absurd piece of bombast the "Prison Thoughts," he could actually reduce his legal "point" and its refutation to blank verse:

> On full intention to repay the whole,
> And in that full intention perfect work
> Free restoration and complete: on wrong
> Or injury to none design'd or wrought,
> I rest my claims.
> Groundless—'tis thundered in my ears—and weak!
> For in the rigid courts of human law
> No restitution wipes away th' offence,
> Nor does intention justify.

make restitution, he very gently pointed out that if excuses of such a kind were to be admitted, it would be a defence for criminals of every kind and degree— for how could the law take notice of what was passing in their minds. Doctor Dodd could scarcely answer for himself that he would have restored the sum. To which the judge might have added, that the restitution on which the prisoner leant so much was *after* his arrest—a step which we may be sure any detected criminal would gladly take, if it was to help him.

At the close of the charge, an ingenious "point" was made by the prisoner's counsel. These were the days when "a flaw" in the indictment was fatal. If the prisoner was *accused* of an offence ever so little differing from the one proved, he escaped. Now, the indictment can be amended on the spot. It was laid in the charge that he had forged an instrument for *seven* hundred pounds annuity; but the bond produced to support that charge had the word seven all blotted, so as to be illegible. The proof and the charge did not therefore correspond. It was a bit of true Old Bailey ingenuity; and the judge admitted its force, but neutralised it by telling the jury it was for them to consider whether the blotted word was meant to represent seven.

They retired. They were only away a few minutes. In a broken voice (it was said "weeping") they brought in their verdict—" GUILTY !" The scene must have been very affecting. The court, the jury, the spectators, were all in tears. A foreigner who was present received an extraordinary impression

of an English judicial proceeding.* The jury recommended him to mercy; but the judges were con-
strained to refuse to second the recommendation, and
bid them apply to the Recorder. The miserable
prisoner was carried away in a crowd of sobbing
friends. It however brought to a close a miserable
day, during which he could not have had a moment's
hope.†

A yet more miserable duty remained—the breaking
the news to the wretched wife, who had sat all day
in a room near the court, expecting news of his fate.

---

* Archenholtz. He was also attracted by the prisoner's noble mien
and appearance.

† In the ill-judged production to which allusion has been made, he
has courage to deal with this situation in such heroics as these:

> Cheerly, my friends, oh cheerly! All is not lost.
> Lo! I have gained *on this important day*
> A victory consummate. . . . On this day,
> My birthday to eternity, I've gain'd
> Dismission from a world . . .
> Ah, little thought ye, prosecutors prompt,
> To do me good like this!

CHAPTER THE NINTH.

PRISON THOUGHTS.

NEWGATE was then very much in the state of the prison to which the good Doctor Primrose was consigned. It was an abomination, and one of the plague-spots of the land, though Mr. James Hanway was even then trying to bring about some amelioration in the condition of the prisoners. But as criminal life was then held so cheap, it was only natural that what ministered to the support of that life should be disregarded. In all the agitation of this terrible change, with death hanging over his head, and his wife just torn from his arms, as the hour for locking up drew near, on the second night of his arrival—a Sunday—how will it be supposed the prisoner spent his hours? In writing rapid, stilted, unprofitable *blank verse*—the mass of weak, vain, ill-judged lines that go to make up "The Prison Thoughts"—a task he continued steadily for five weeks. A piece which, taken with its surrounding associations, with

its style, matter, length, and quality, makes up one
of the most extraordinary performances in the world.
It is absolutely unique. Can we conceive a man of
known refinement and of "elegant tastes" plunged
suddenly into the most horrible of gaols, with the
gallows in the distance, and the consciousness that
his name was in every man's mouth in London—a
man of epicurean sensitiveness, reduced to misery
under every circumstance of horror—can we conceive
him, not merely preserving his reason, but sitting
down to scribble hundreds of blank verses—lines of
the very poorest quality? It could not have been
mere dull insensibility; we must, with more likelihood, set it to the account of that old theatrical taste
and vanity—putting himself before the town as the
romantic and persecuted Doctor, whose gentle verses
would be read in drawing-rooms by moistened female
eyes.*

* Prefixed to the MS. was found a note, dated April 23, which
shows clearly what his aim was:

"April 23, 1777.

"I began these Thoughts merely from the impression of my mind,
without plan, purpose, or motive, more than the situation and state of
my soul. I continued them on a thoughtful and regular plan: and I
have been enabled wonderfully—in a state, which in better days I
should have supposed would have destroyed all power of reflection—to
bring them nearly to a conclusion. I dedicate them to God, and to the
reflecting serious amongst my fellow-creatures; and I bless the Almighty
for the ability to go through them, amidst the terrors of this dire
place, and bitter anguish of my disconsolate mind!

"The thinking will easily pardon all inaccuracies, as I am neither
able nor *willing* to read over these melancholy lines with a *curious* or
critical eye! They are imperfect, but the language of the heart; and,
had I time and inclination, might and should be improved.

"But——!   "W. D."

This clap-trap finish and theatrical breaking off at the word "*But*——"
is truly characteristic.

The old vices that shipwrecked him all through his old life leavens this production. The cantos are labelled *The Trial, The Retrospect*, &c.; and every verse furnishes a peg on which to hang some personal reference to his private glories. There are notes that show off his erudition; references to theatres, pictures, travels in France, deceased comedians —interrupted every moment with unworthy appeals for mercy, whining Jeremiads over his fate, and the exaggerated self-laudation of ostentatious penitence and complacent conversion. These "Prison Thoughts" are a sure index of that "unsoundness" which may be traced all through the pattern of his life, and which threw off, even to the last hour of his life, those wild flashy lights, which are wholly inconsistent with sincere, steady repentance.

The man that could quote Milton and "my hapless ancestor Overbury," and bid the reader in a note "See my Sermon on the Injustice, &c."—"See my Elegy on the Death of Frederick Prince of Wales, Poems, p. 63," was scarcely in the overwhelmed and repentant condition he professed himself to be in.

More singular, however, were his complacent proclamations of a virtuous life, and a boastful enumeration of all the books he had written, and the charities he had established.

Did he think of his novel, "The Sisters," when he said that his pen, "However humble, ne'er has traced a line Of tendency immoral"? Or did he think of his confession, "My life has for some years back been *dreadfully erroneous*"? More curious, too, his forgetfulness, when he proceeded to rebuke the "Men of God Who crowd the levee, theatre, *or court, Foremost*

in each amusement's idle walk: *Of Vice and Vanity
the sportive scorn*,"—lines which, to a nicety, describe
himself. In the case of "aged friends" enjoying
youthful follies, he owns that, "with due shame,
and sorrow, and regret—O pardon me the mighty
wrong," he had sat by silent, and, with "a pitying
eye," left these excesses unreproved.

The view that Johnson took of the false "Prison
Thoughts" is quite consistent with the true and practical view he took of its author's case. He could
hardly bring himself to look at it, and it was not
until Boswell had read some portions that he gave
his verdict on it: "Pretty well, if you are disposed
to like it." When he heard some more read, he liked
it better. This was his toleration for the verses. But
he broke out loudly when he came to the Prayer for
.the King at the end, and to other elaborate pieces of
sentiment. Though he felt for the man, he scorned
the theatrical colouring, and the attempt to invest a
coarse crime with a spicy tinsel of romance. "Sir,"
he said, bluntly, "do you think a man, the night before
he is to be hanged, cares for a royal family, though he
may have composed this prayer?"

Never did condemned prisoner meet with such indulgence. From the governor, Mr. Akerman, down-
wards—happily a humane official, who was the friend
of many notable men in London—he received every
allowance short of freedom. He had a private room,
books, fire, and all comforts. His friends found
money, and supplied him with everything. But nothing could shut out the grim and terrible associations
of the place. Through the walls, the horrid riot, the

awful saturnalia, arising from the promiscuous herding together of prisoners of every shade of crime, came to his ears. He began his "Prison Thoughts" at eight o'clock—"the hour when they lock up this dismal place;" and then, and even up to midnight, was shocked and appalled by "the din of rough voices, shrieking imprecations, roaring bursts of loud obstreperous laughter, and strange choirs of gutturals," which were heard even at midnight. The more hardened criminals had a habit of clanking their chains, as if in wanton defiance of authority. In short, it was a terrible medley of horrible sounds, dreadful to a sensitive mind. More chilling still, was the booming of St. Sepulchre's bell, close by, which, "by long and pious custom," was tolled the night before an execution, for the purpose of announcing to criminals that their end was near; and as Monday was execution-day, this lugubrious memento was heard nearly every Sunday night—a ceremony for which the charitable citizen, Richard Dowe, had left a foundation.*

* Another part of this custom used to be that the "Bellman" came under the window of Newgate, as near to the prisoner's cell as he could, and after giving "twelve solemn towles" with a little handbell, repeated this quaint and solemn warning:

> All you that in the condemn'd cell do lie,
> Prepare you, for to-morrow you shall die.
> Watch all and pray, the hour is drawing near,
> When you before th' Almighty must appear.
> Examine well yourselves, in time repent,
> That you may not t' eternal flames be sent.
> And when St. 'Pulchre's bell to-morrow tolls,
> The Lord have mercy on your souls.
>   Past twelve o'clock.

CHAPTER THE TENTH.

SENTENCE.

BUT now another actor was to step upon the stage, and a great massive soul to range itself beside that poor, unsound, shrinking nature, overshadow it, and lift it into something like dignity. But for the brave, honest, manly, and even chivalrous countenance of Johnson—had not the " Grand Old Samuel" so resolutely, earnestly, and unselfishly—for the interference brought him no credit—lent him his strong arm—the last scenes of the last days of the miserable man would have lost even their decent semblance of pathetic interest. Of all Johnson's many acts of Christian charity, there are none we can look to which show in so noble a light as this aid to the doomed parson.

Hawkins says boldly that they had never met. But this is incorrect. Johnson recollected perfectly having been in his company once, and relished him as little as he did " the man Sterne." The two natures were indeed as unlikely to mix as oil and water.

Johnson shrank from the flash and tinsel of the ecclesiastical macaroni. Johnson did not well recollect
the occasion, but he made a very great impression on
Dodd, who, the very next day, sent a perfect photograph of the "great moralist" to his friend Parkhurst—the same who had been so impressed after
dinner by Dodd's soliloquy upon divine things.

"I spent yesterday afternoon," he wrote, "with
Johnson, the celebrated author of 'The Rambler,'
who is of all others the oddest and most peculiar
fellow I ever saw. He is six feet high, has a violent
convulsion in his head, and his eyes are distorted. He
speaks roughly and loud, listens to no man's opinion
—thoroughly pertinacious of his own. Good sense
flows from him in all he utters, and he seems possessed of a prodigious fund of knowledge, which he
is not at all reserved of communicating; but in a
manner so obstinate, *ungenteel,* and boorish, as renders
it disagreeable and unsatisfactory."

He little dreamt, then, what profit, or what sort of
help, he was to obtain from "the ungenteel" nature.
No wonder the fashionable clergyman was repelled by
the moralist's bluff manner.

The feeling that brought him to Dodd's assistance
is quite intelligible. With his almost morbid terror
of death, even under its most ordinary condition, and
of all that was associated with death, this snatching
away of a man, who seemed removed from it by sound
health and long years and the refinements of society,
must have had something horrible and appalling.
We can fancy his shrinking from the whole episode,
or thinking of it with groans and sore convulsions of

K

his great figure. And when we think how manly and independent he was—how reluctant to canvass any one of rank or influence—how little he chose to run the risk of being unsuccessful in any undertaking—above all, how he believed in the King—it must be said that the earnest, eager way in which he took up this unhappy case, makes one of his many claims to that affection and respect with which we regard him. But when we consider the natures of the two men, as opposed as fire and water, as repugnant as truth and falsehood—since he was a man whom, if he had crossed his path in life, Johnson would have scorned and exposed, and stripped of his tinsel and shams,—this makes the sacrifice yet more extraordinary. Above this, aid was given with a tenderness and delicacy not to be reckoned on in one who was popularly said to be " a bear," but who had, indeed, only the skin of the bear.

It is illustrative of this morbid feeling on Johnson's side that he could not bring himself to visit Dodd in his prison. To him there would have been something almost appalling in the sight of a fellow-creature, full of health and strength, lying in a gaol under sentence. With truth he said, " It would have done *me* more harm than good to *him*." Once, indeed, Dodd expressed a desire to see him, but did not press it further.

Great hopes were entertained of the law point. Exertions were still being made outside—faint, however, as compared with the exertions to be made later. More petitions were signed. Nearly three months passed over, and it came to the middle of May, when eleven of the judges—the Chief Justice De Grey being absent—met at their chambers in Serjeants' Inn, and discussed the question of Robertson's evidence. They were unanimous in holding that it was legally admitted.

The ground was fast slipping from beneath him. It shows how deep was the interest in the matter, that on that very same day a privy council was held at St. James's, at which Lords Mansfield, North, Hertford, Hillsborough, Carlisle, and others, with the Lord Chancellor, assisted, where they debated upwards of an hour on the propriety of suffering the law to take its course. There can be no question but that Lord Mansfield formed a harsh and adverse opinion from the very outset. This was the popular belief; and it is confirmed by a bitter newspaper remark of nearly the same date, which shows him taking then a strong line of severity to the wretched prisoners who were rotting away in the Thames hulks. To the same privy council, Lord Weymouth was seen to go in, carrying "a bundle of petitions;" but no decision was arrived at.

Never was an unhappy prisoner of such sensibility to pass through such trials. He must have suffered the bitterness of death many times; and the dramatic forms of mental torture seem to have been ingeniously multiplied to increase his agony. On the 14th of May he was carried to the bar of the Old Bailey, and again exposed to a crowded and curious court. The judge told the result of the argument, and that he had sent for him to give him this early notice to prepare for his sentence. This was another scene for

K 2

the unhappy prisoner, who would only murmur a few words as to his having perfect reliance on the equity and wisdom of the judges. His piteous groans then filled the court, and when he was taken away he fell senseless on the floor of the dock.

The Old Bailey sessions were now at hand, and on the 26th of May he was brought up to receive sentence. This was to be another scene. He was asked what he had to say. He faltered, tried to get out a few words with clenched hands and streaming eyes, and tottered. Then the Recorder proceeded with his duty, and addressed him: "Doctor William Dodd!" A sensible and almost sympathising address, in which he plainly glanced at the prisoner's appeals to the public. He was glad to see this expression of sorrow. "But one thing I wish you to avoid—that is, *any palliation* of your crime. From your education and abilities you had no excuse. By *no means, therefore,* go about to extenuate your offence, but prepare yourself for the awful event." This was a very significant hint. The miserable divine being asked what he had to say why it should not be passed upon him, he delivered what was called "an animated and pathetic address," written for him by the manly hand of his new friend. It merely touched, very lightly and judiciously, on the merits of a past life—on the sudden fall—and moderately took credit for thirty years passed in charity. Can we not hear the voice of Johnson in this passage :

"I have fallen from reputation which ought to have made me cautious ; and from a fortune which ought to have given me content. I am sunk at once into poverty and scorn; my name and my crime fill the ballads—the sport of the thoughtless, and the triumph of the wicked."

It was truly Johnsonian to say he did not mean to be " finally fraudulent," which expressed in two words all the refinements and excuses about meaning to restore the money. And with this pathetic close it ended:

" Let not a little time be denied me, in which I may, by meditation and contrition, be prepared to stand at the tribunal of Omnipotence, and support the presence of that Judge who shall distribute to all according to their works, who will receive to pardon the repenting sinner, and from whom the merciful shall obtain mercy.

" For these reasons, amidst shame and misery, I yet wish to live; and most humbly entreat that I may be recommended by your lordship to the clemency of his Majesty."

Yet it may be questioned if these studied periods of weighty English would have been as effective for an audience, as the agitated, unprepared address fresh from Dodd's own heart. But Johnson wisely saw that all was dependent on argument; and there is real skill all through these papers, in the way the very delicate topics are put. He was then led away quite helpless, and groaning with unutterable anguish, and exclaiming in the most lamentable moanings, " Lord Jesus receive my soul!" After the excitement had subsided, Eliot, the foreman of the jury, presented their petition, saying that the severe course taken on the day of trial had filled them with the deepest con-

cern—that they then " retained a wish to serve him,"
but finding themselves obliged to pronounce him
guilty, there was no other course or hope but to implore mercy for him.

For his assistance he wrote Johnson a letter of
fervent gratitude. He said he could not conceive,
" my ever dear sir," the use that speech " on the
awful day" had been to him ; " I experienced every
hour some good effect from it." Johnson was busy,
too, composing a sermon for him—" your kind and
intended favour" he calls it. " I am sure, had I your
sentiments constantly to deliver for them, in all their
mighty force and *power, not a soul could be left uncon-
verted*"—a strain of compliment that must have jarred
on Johnson. He winds up by calling him " *the first
man* of our times."*

---

* As to Dodd's " point" about not being " finally fraudulent," it is
curious that the very subject should have been discussed at the Mitre
Tavern some nine years before. BOSWELL: " I cannot think that his"
(Rousseau's) " intention was bad." JOHNSON: " Sir, that will not do.
We cannot prove any man's intention to be bad. You may shoot a
man through the head, and say you intended to miss him; but the judge
will order you to be hanged. *An alleged want of intention, when evil is
committed, will not be allowed in a court of justice.*" This summary,
contained in a sentence or two, is far more forcible than the judge's
more lengthy exposition of the law.

CHAPTER THE ELEVENTH.

" THE UNFORTUNATE DOCTOR DODD."

FROM this time his life became, as Walpole put it,
"a series of protracted horrors." It was more a
flurry and a fever than a life; and in this fever the
sands of life were fast slipping away. Nor was this
agitation inside the prison only; the whole country
was in a ferment. Monster petitions were presented
from various sources.

The Methodists, to whom he was not thought to
be partial, took up his case with extraordinary eagerness; a petition was drawn up by Johnson—"one of
the most energetic compositions ever seen," says
Hawkins; conceived in a tone of lowly contrition,
praying for mercy for "the most distressed and
wretched of your Majesty's subjects, *William Dodd.*"

The petition was engrossed upon a large sheet of
parchment, in an exquisite specimen of caligraphy,
by " Tomkins, of Sermon-lane," one of the most
famous penmen that ever lived. He made his way to

the Doctor's cell, and offered these charitable services, such as they were—which were gratefully accepted. The poor Doctor was, indeed, likely enough to be grateful for assistance of any degree or kind. At the Shakspeare Tavern, on one of these evenings, Henderson the actor, Richardson the scene-painter, Wilson the sculptor, and some more, were sitting talking over the great subject, when Cipriani and Mortimer came in. Tomkins exhibited this specimen of his art, and proposed that Mortimer and Cipriani should paint allegorical images of Mercy and Justice, surrounded by his flourishes. This idea amused the company, but their hilarity sent the gentleman away offended.*

The petition was taken round. Everybody canvassed for signatures. The parish officers were seen performing this duty clad in deep mourning. A friend of his, before alluded to, Doctor Kennedy, was indefatigable. A boy long recollected three gentlemen coming round Soho with the roll of paper and inkhorns, collecting names. These were the elder Sheridan, Dudley Bate, and Dr. Kennedy.† They called on Horne Tooke. He told them, with rough humour, that he liked their errand, and thought it would do, because people would take them for tax-gatherers, and be so agreeably disappointed that they would sign readily.

The petition—the result of their efforts—was a remarkable one. It was thirty-seven yards and a quarter long, and contained twenty-three thousand signatures, the first of which was the foreman of the jury, who

---

* Angelo's Memoirs.   † Ibid.

prayed his Majesty "to consider that he is truly distressed at finding the Doctor included in the dead list." It was called the petition of the gentry, merchants, and traders of London. Surely, as Johnson well said, "the voice of the public, when it calls so loudly for mercy, ought to be heard!"

All the while paragraphs in the newspapers, in the same key, about "the unfortunate Doctor Dodd," kept up the excitement. Johnson himself wrote some editorial remarks in one journal, in which were some admirable Rambler-like arguments, the strongest of which was, "that no arbiter of life and death has ever been censured for granting the life of a criminal to honest and powerful solicitation." He also prepared one for Mrs. Dodd, to be laid at the feet of the queen. Earl Percy, then very popular with the people for his part in the American question, was got to present the petition. Another petition was also prepared by the same hand, to be sent up by the common council, which, however, he said they had "mended."

With horrors thus gathering, and the pious, outside, mourning his fate, and he himself crushed by the recollection of that exposure in public court, it must have been weeks before he could shut it out from his eyes. Yet the old spots were not to be changed so readily. Even in Newgate, through all that outside plating of grief and misery, the old macaroni metal was to make its way through. About this time Mr. William Woodfall received an earnest appeal from him, requesting a visit at the prison. Thinking that this had reference to the insertion of some paragraph in his *Morning Chronicle*, he set off, with some reluctance, however. On entering, he began with embarrassment the usual platitudes of condolence, but was at once interrupted by the Doctor, who said he had sent for him on quite a different matter. He then pulled out——a comedy!—" Sir Roger de Coverley"—on which he said he was anxious to have Mr. Woodfall's opinion ; and further, his interest with the managers to get it brought forward. Woodfall was shocked at this insensibility, the more so as Mr. Akerman, the keeper of the gaol, had just told him of the arrival of the order for execution. Naturally, he endeavoured to divert the prisoner's mind from so unsuitable a topic ; but the Doctor turned the matter off repeatedly, saying, "O, they will never hang me." Much relieved at this business-like proposal, the printer agreed with alacrity, and took it away with him. He, later, suggested a few alterations, which were adopted. It found its way to Mr. Harris, of Covent Garden, where, no doubt, it perished by fire, with others of greater merit, but not so curious in origin.*

Even from the gaol we get hints of that old unsoundness of life ; and while writing those complacent blank panegyrics of himself and his virtues, he received a strange appeal from Toplady, the Methodist, which is very significant : " Reverend Sir," it ran, " believe me when I assure you that I take

---

* This story is too characteristic to be rejected. Woodfall was a man of integrity, and we have it from him in no less than two shapes. See *Biographia Dramatica*, article " Sir Roger de Coverley," and Taylor's *Recollections*.

the liberty which I now take, neither from want
of tenderness nor of respect," and then he proceeds to
recal to Doctor Dodd's mind a certain " Mrs. G——,
whose circumstances are *considerably reduced and embarrassed, through the unsuspecting confidence she re-
posed in your veracity, justice, and honour.*" He con-
jures him pathetically, " by every sacred and moral
consideration, not to depart this world without repay-
ing as much of *that iniquitous debt* as you possibly
can.   I say," he goes on, " before you depart this
world, for it is but too well understood that there is
not a single ray of hope from any one quarter of your
avoiding the utmost effect of that terrible sentence
which impends." He then hinted at the Doctor's
supposed employment of "writing notes to Shakspeare,"
a rumour which may have arisen from his being busy
with the " Prison Thoughts."*

The "iniquitous debt" was clearly a breach of
trust of some kind; whether it was ever discharged,
we have no means of knowing.

Years and years before he had known Romaine,
the popular " minister," and had been assisted by him in
his Hebrew studies.   When the Doctor rose in the
world, he told Romaine that he would be glad to
see him privately at his house, but that he hoped
not to be acknowledged by Romaine in public.   An
acquaintance on such terms was naturally declined.
Now, a friend coming from Newgate, met Romaine
near the Old Bailey, and they began to talk of the
prisoner.   Romaine said he was sorry to hear Dodd

* Toplady's Works.

was visited by all " sorts of light and trifling people."
The other, much hurt, refuted the charge, though it
is to be suspected there was some truth in it, on
which Romaine promised to visit Dodd. He was
afterwards asked if he " who knew so much of the
human heart" thought Dodd a real penitent ? and he
replied, " I hope he is a real penitent, but there is a
great difference between saying and *feeling* ' God be
merciful to me a sinner.'"

Allowing a little margin for the intolerance with
which a man like Romaine would look on a man like
Dodd, and with the versified penitence of the " Prison
Thoughts" before us, this seems about a just view of
the prisoner's state of mind. An admiring lady friend
of Romaine's said that the sentiment ought to be put
in letters of gold.

Inflammatory pamphlets were printed, addressed
personally to the prosecutors—Fletcher and Peach—
and abusing them in unmeasured terms. One of
them concluded: " On the whole, if Dodd be hanged,
you must allow me the liberty of supplicating your
God to receive his soul, and by a reformation in the
manners of his survivors to render them deserving of
His mercy."

Never was there such an absorbing topic of conversation. He was a friend of a certain good but
odd Doctor Kennedy, who was the friend of Foote,
Sterne, and Garrick. For this gentleman Gainsborough had painted a fine picture of a fashionable
Black who was then the town talk, and it is a slight
evidence of Dodd's power of attracting friends, that

Doctor Kennedy presented this picture to the Duchess of Queensberry, in the hope of getting her to forward his friend's interests. Now, at this crisis, he exerted himself afresh. When the petition came to be signed, he went round and canvassed all his friends. In short, at every house the conversation came round to that one topic, and the tone of the conversation was to that one chant, " Poor Doctor Dodd."*

Yet, those who could not reach him personally, contrived to reach him in another way ; and the unfortunate man was persecuted by a flood of letters of a "most unchristian, horrid, and cruel nature," poured in on him without ceasing, and yet signed, " A Christian," " A Lady," or " A Christian Brother." Officious zeal prompted other appeals to him " to be converted." The only one of this class that seems to have been acceptable, were the really affectionate appeals of Miss Bosanquet, one of his old friends and admirers, and whose letters were really kind, thoughtful, practical, and consolatory.

* In the old Newgate Calendar is given a portrait of the Doctor as he appeared " writing his Prison Thoughts." The dungeon is the true stage dungeon : he has on enormous fetters, and a pitcher of water is in the corner. The Doctor fared very differently.

CHAPTER THE TWELFTH.

THE CONVICT'S ADDRESS.

FROM this time forth, he was to be spoken of as
" the unfortunate Doctor Dodd," everywhere, in con-
versations as well as in newspapers—a title, Sir J.
Hawkins remarks, in one of his very few just observations, which contributed a good deal to send abroad
a false idea of his situation, as though he had been
altogether the victim of circumstances. The name
filled the air. He was the universal subject in club,
coffee-house, and drawing-room. It was mentioned
with commiseration.

The town appears to have ranged itself on the two
sides, and to have taken the question up with the
heat and fury of partisanship. Nothing illustrates
this better than the tone of the little Memoirs, which,
both before and after his end, went fluttering into
the air; those against him conceived in a bitterly
hostile and, considering the season, almost indecent
spirit; those for him, in a smooth and exaggerated

panegyric, ludicrously untrue, representing his whole life as one growing current of virtue and charming piety. These were, to some extent, the justification of the former class, for there were numbers who knew how false the picture was, and that his life could not be twisted into that of some pious Methodist minister, whose good deeds and sayings were to be published for the edification of the faithful. As an instance of this oily euphuism, his success as a good "drawing" preacher was thus accounted for: "Hence the beauty of holiness appears so enticing in a young man, and whenever he preached the church was crowded." In the same fashion his early indiscretions were varnished over, or rather wholly dropped out, and he appears, during the awkward season of his early London escapade, and during the time he was busy embodying scenes from a wild life in his novel, as a sort of virtuous and overworked curate.

It was a proof of his favour in the City, when the Court of Common Council met expressly to consider the propriety of petitioning for him. In this assembly there was about the same division of party as there was outside. Deputy Jones pleading his cause in a most pathetic speech, showing how the good he had done outbalanced any evil, and introducing secretaries to the various charities as witnesses in his favour. Alderman Woolridge, with good sense, questioned the propriety of the course they were taking as quite unprecedented, though he added he heartily wished him all mercy. To whom a Deputy Fisher ingeniously replied—taking a truly "City view" of the matter—that there could be no impropriety in the matter, as the forgery laws were made sanguinary purposely for the commercial world. Hence they, as representing the City of London, the very heart of commerce, might fairly ask for lenity. The petition was adopted finally, though with reluctance.

This application was prepared by Johnson, though he afterwards seemed to complain of their having "mended it." *

One of the great subjects of conversation outside was the behaviour of Lord Chesterfield. It was believed he could have saved his tutor; and certainly in those times, when a rich and influential nobleman could do much that was illegal, it seemed likely that some method could have been found to check the law's progress. It is hard for us to know, at this distance of time, what *could* have been done; but it has been shown that he was all but helpless in the matter. The public made no

---

* Strange to say, the City petitioners marvellously improved the composition, both in sense and force, as will be seen at a glance, by comparing a passage or two. Johnson wrote, "and we have reason to believe has executed his ministry with great fidelity and efficacy;" which, besides the uncertainty of the assertion, is a little too general. For this the "menders" substituted the more forcible, "which in many instances has produced the happiest effect." Johnson wrote, "that he has been the first initiator, *or* a very earnest and active promoter of several modes of useful charity." Meaning to convey with nice logical accuracy that he had founded some charities, and forwarded others which he had no share in founding. The common councillors removed the uncertainty of the disjunctive, substituting an "and." They inserted an humble "encouraged by your Majesty's well-known clemency," substituted "not an unworthy object of pardon" for "not unfit object," and pruned down many of Johnson's correct but clumsy "thats."

such allowance; and his share in the proceeding was long recollected. When he said, jocularly, to the well-known Colonel Berkeley, who had had several encounters on Hounslow Heath, "Berkeley, how long is it since you shot a highwayman?" the other replied, promptly, "How long is it since *you* hung a parson?"* Seven years later he was named ambassador to Madrid; set off, and stayed nearly two years in the country round Marseilles, drawing his salary all the time. This job caused loud complaints. He, however, was a great favourite of the king's, having "pleasing and lively manners," which, perhaps, he learnt from his luckless tutor. To improve this royal intercourse, he actually for years gave up his fine seat at Bretby, and took a little place near Windsor. He lived into the year 1815.

On Friday, June 6, was witnessed, in the chapel of Newgate, a very strange spectacle, and one of a very tragic significance. The convicts were all gathered there; and from the pulpit a sermon was delivered to them by a clergyman who was himself a convict—and a condemned convict. It must have been an awful and deeply impressive sight. And indeed we can conceive that nothing could have more weight, or have been more profitable for the abandoned miscellany of convicts about him, than some earnest words addressed to them from one who was addressing them, as it were, half way out of his grave. A truly sincere penitent would have eagerly

---

* This story was told long ago by Wraxall, who had it from Colonel Berkeley, through Lord Sandwich. He is now confirmed by Colonel Berkeley's son, Mr. Grantley Berkeley.

L

seized on the opportunity. But it looks as though this hapless Dodd had clutched at it only as another possible plank to which he might cling, and get to shore. Johnson was made to write the sermon.* It was then carefully altered, pruned, and added to, in Newgate—and even furnished with notes; for the truth was, it was intended to be preached, not to the miserable convicts in the gaol, but to the great London congregation outside. All this looks like some of the old theatricals; but still, in such dark and desperate straits, it is hard to deal severely with him. Very shortly "The Convict's Address to his Unhappy Brethren" (a melodramatic title) was published, and greedily read.

Great hopes were now begun to be entertained, and not without reason. At times his fate did seem to rest on, literally, the turn of a card. It was debated many times. The king could not make up his mind. Walpole represents Lord Mansfield as playing a most malignant part. It was artfully put, as a question between that dreadful and dangerous entity, "the people" and the royal power. The people were growing very daring, and this looked like pressure. It was said, even before the judges had given their opinion, he had declared that the law should be carried out.

* Johnson began very strikingly, " You see with what confusion I now stand before you. No more in the pulpit of instruction, but in the humble seat with yourselves." Dodd, however, weakened it by intruding a passage preceding it. He also added " notes"—a shape of his almost incorrigible vanity. Johnson was naturally proud of a compliment of Miss Porter's: " When I read Dr. Dodd's Sermon to the Prisoners, I said Dr. Johnson could not make a better."

It has been popularly said that the king had declared that if he pardoned Dodd, he would have considered that he had murdered the Perreaus—two forgers who had been executed the year before. This was actually imputed to Johnson, which was improbable on the face of it; but with more likelihood was said by Hawkins to have appeared in a newspaper.

It had now come to June. The time was drawing on. The exertions were being redoubled and made with almost frantic ardour. In the second week of this month the Recorder "made his report to his Majesty of such prisoners as were lying under sentence of death in Newgate—viz. Doctor William Dodd and Joseph Harris." It is a horrible testimony to the barbarous code of the times, that Joseph Harris's offence was the robbing of a stage-coach passenger of *" two half guineas and about seven shillings."* But no one seems to have ever dreamt of interfering for the life of luckless Joseph Harris.

On the 15th of June the privy council assembled, and deliberated for the last time on the case of the several prisoners. A final decision was at last arrived at: and it was to be read in the London papers of that evening that a warrant had been made out for the execution of Doctor Dodd, on Friday, the 27th.

CHAPTER THE THIRTEENTH.

THE PREROGATIVE OF MERCY.

THERE is reason to believe that it was Lord Mansfield who really decided the question of Dodd's fate. It was the popular impression, and it was, besides, exactly the view that we should expect a man of such rigid constitutional views as *he* entertained, to take.[*] Walpole, too, had heard it on good authority; and Wraxall had been told of it by one who was actually present at the council. Walpole had heard that he had "indecently" declared for execution before even the judges had given judgment. The story went that the king had been long undecided and irresolute, then had finally turned to the Chief Justice and had asked his opinion, and on finding that he was against mercy, had taken up the pen without a word and signed the dreadful paper.[†] Dodd himself had

---

[*] Lord Campbell, in his Lives, passes over Mansfield's share in this transaction without a word of notice.

[†] In ordinary criminal cases there was no regular warrant signed, and the judge merely wrote in a column opposite the prisoner's name

an instinct of this fatal influence, and on the 11th
of June got Johnson to address him a pathetic letter,
signed, "Your lordship's most humble suppliant,
William Dodd.* This pathetic appeal had no effect
on the cold heart of the Chief Justice.

And here in this place naturally arises the question—which in those times arose and was debated
with such heat and eagerness—Should the king have
spared Dodd? Taking the case in all its bearings,
the temptation, the little injury that was done, his
profession and station, we may safely come to the
conclusion that he would have been a fit object for
royal mercy. Not but that it might have been
forcibly argued that the bloody code of those days
required at least impartiality in its administration;
and it must not be forgotten that the very sessions at
which Dodd was tried, a wretched man was sentenced
to death *for washing a halfpenny over to make it pass
for a shilling,* and a woman to be burnt in the hand
for assisting in the same offence!

The bloody code, as then administered, was marked
by indecent haste and carelessness; frightful mistakes
arising out of that carelessness; a cold-blooded indifference in those in authority, and revolting but

the words (not even at full length) "sus. per col." This little memo-
randum was all the authority the sheriff had to act on, for taking
away a man's life. It is characteristic that at this time, in matters
of distraint, or anything affecting the *taking away of property,* the law
actually bristled with points, and the nicest scrutiny was made into the
question of authority. Human life was far cheaper.

* It is in the same key as the other letters. It escaped Boswell,
Croker, and other commentators on Johnson's writings, and is only to
be found in Archenholtz's Travels.

natural callousness on the part of the convicted. It has been said, indeed, and accepted generally because said so often, that this severity actually frustrated its own end, and that juries used to acquit from a disinclination to send men to death for such light offences. But this accounts for but a small margin, and we need only look at the newspapers of the time, and the epitomes of the bloody work of the circuits that found their way into magazines, to see what a wholesale judicial butchery went on. "We hanged," says Mr. Philips, "for everything—for a shilling, for five shillings, for forty shillings, for five pounds, for cutting down a sapling." A young woman of nineteen, whose husband had been pressed, and who had been starving in consequence, took up a bit of coarse linen on a counter, and laid it down again when she was noticed; and for this was hung with her child at her breast. Reading of such horrors and not interfering, with what equity could the king have yielded to influential pressure and spare the life of the genteel clergyman who had forged a bond of such large amount?

Yet we cannot think there was any thought of the man who washed over the shilling, and who only made one of the doomed herd who were carted away to Tyburn of Monday mornings. The king, indeed, said, "If I pardon Dodd, I shall have murdered the Perreaus"—wealthy traders in Dodd's own station, who had been executed for forgery also, a year or two before.*

---

* This royal argument has been often commented on as weak. But there is really some force in it. If the reasons against mercy were as

But the truth was, there was a popular agitation abroad, and a sort of clamorous pressure, which, it being now only a few years before the revolutionary times, seemed a little alarming to the advisers of the Crown. It was action on the part of *the people*, which at that time, however constitutional, was looked upon as dangerous. There can be little doubt—especially considering Lord Mansfield's share in the matter—that this was the motive that guided the issue. Something, too, must be placed to the account of that stubborn purpose and almost mulish obstinacy of the " great George" the Third, which broke out in dealings with his ministers, and in dealings with his children; and which, perhaps, made him resist, because every one was appealing to him to give way. Exactly twenty years before an admiral had been hanged to " encourage the others," and it was now almost a pity that general criticism on Dodd's approaching fate could not be compressed into another and as happy a saying of Voltaire's.

This, " the most amiable prerogative of the Crown," as Blackstone calls it, might indeed have been fairly exercised. It would have been gracious, for there was, as Johnson put it, a general desire that the prisoner's life should be spared.

It was exactly the sort of case where the king might indulge himself with the luxury of forgiveness, which the law allows him, as an almost arbitrary privilege. This is the true view of this prerogative; namely, its being *a personal* act of the sovereign's; and it is in

strong in one case as in the other, and Dodd was spared, it would certainly have scarcely an impartial air.

this view that the Recorder of London had to *report*
to the king the names of all the prisoners under
sentence, and had " to take his pleasure" thereon. This
power, which is quite intelligible, has gradually been
delegated to the Home Secretary, who exercises an
irregular and utterly anomalous jurisdiction; review-
ing trials, altering sentences, and becoming, in fact, a
sort of " Cassation Judge;" only a cassation judge
who has had no legal training, and is bound by no
precedents or fixed procedure. We can see what a
distortion this is of the " amiable prerogative" granted
to the king. The question is too long to be entered
on here; but the true course would be to establish a
Court of Criminal Appeal, who would do in a legal
and regular way what the Secretary of State is
allowed to do so illegally and irregularly, and restore
to the sovereign the more limited but gracious exer-
cise of his old prerogative.

The distinction may be illustrated by an instance
or two. At the sessions when Dodd was tried, was
found guilty and sentenced to death a Spaniard who,
in a fit of frantic jealousy, had stabbed his mistress.
Supposing the existence of a proper Court of Criminal
Appeal, the course would have been as follows : Had
the evidence been circumstantial, and there had been
doubts as to whether it supported the verdict, an
appeal could have been made to the Criminal Court,
and a new trial ordered. Was the case considered
murder, but yet under circumstances of some allowance, the appeal could have been to the " gracious"
feeling of the king, who might have pardoned or commuted. Thus there would be two distinct provinces.

Thus the cases of Kirwan and Jessie Maclachlan would not have remained monuments of inconsistency in our criminal annals. If there had been such a court, the grave doubts as to the weight of the evidence that convicted them, might have been taken there, examined by skilled men familiar with the true tests of evidence, and accepted or rejected as they deserved to be. And we would not have had a wild jurisdiction interposing to save the accused from death, by an interference utterly illogical. The whole has, in short, grown into a tribunal that is both secret and incapable (because uninstructed)—about two of the worst qualities that could infect any earthly tribunal. It is mere accident that has saved the administration of criminal justice from disgraceful en-tanglement.

Suppose, in the recent case of Müller, some *really* grave evidence in his favour had been brought to light after his conviction—so important as to require serious investigation, yet not conclusive as to the point of guilt or innocence — how does this irregular tribunal act? Call in the aid of the judges who tried the case—as was actually done. But how are *they* entitled to re-try a case which should properly go to a jury? And supposing that they report that the evidence is of importance on the side of the accused, the tribunal of the Home Office will have either to grant a free pardon—to which the convict is not entitled—or, which it will most probably do, enter into a compromise with him and commute the sentence to penal servitude. This is, in fact, the unworthy device by which the system is at present saved from exposure. Some doubt arises after the trial; the prisoner cannot be pardoned, and is too glad to be let off with a mitigated punishment, unmerited if he be *legally* innocent, and too light if he be guilty. In the recent cases of Wright and of Townley, the same remark might have been made as was made by the king in the case of Dodd and the Perreaus.

But a case still more in point is the recent one of Dr. Smethurst, who, it will be recollected, was found guilty of poisoning Miss Bankes. Substantial evidence turned up after the trial, the weight of which seriously affected the verdict. In a civil case, how would such a matter be dealt with? A conditional order for a new trial would be applied for and granted; later, the conditional order would be argued, the matter investigated by several judges, the evidence carefully weighed, and finally a new trial granted. But in Smethurst's case—a case regarding life and death—a Home Secretary, a layman, goes through all these processes himself. True, he has assistance, and calls in the aid of the judge who tried the case, and these two authorities take on themselves the unconstitutional duty of re-trying the case and setting aside the verdict of a jury. True, the king can pardon or mitigate punishment, and this appears to be done under cover of his authority, but the king cannot do what is done by this process, overhaul the proceedings of a court—weigh evidence, and set aside a verdict because against evidence. He may extend mercy, because the case is what is called "a hard one," because there are "extenuating circumstances," but not because he thinks *it should be tried differently.*

CHAPTER THE FOURTEENTH.

LAST DAYS.

THE miserable wife had a room in Ludgate-hill, so as to be near her husband. She came to him every day. Every night, after he was ordered for execution, he used to write her a letter. She was a true comfort in these days of horror. The house in Argyle-street had been seized on and almost wrecked under the bills of sale. A gentleman who lived till lately, recollected being present at the auction of the furniture, and found the drawing-room table piled up with letters, lying open there, signed by the most famous names of the day.* These were sold with the "elegant French wines" which were such a feature at the Doctor's entertainments.

Even at this stage we see the unhappy man busy with what seems his old intriguing, and though his "Convict's Address" was said to have displeased the Methodists, they to the end made unusual exertions in his behalf. He received the religious assistance of

* Taylor.

a Moravian minister; and it does almost seem as
though he were in some sort bidding for the enormous
Methodist interest outside, by coquetting a little with
their doctrines.

Up to this moment there had been great hope. A
belief had got abroad that he would not be included
in the order. The crowd of well-meaning friends
buoyed him up with the assurance that it was almost
impossible. One, even more cruelly injudicious than
the rest, had accepted a false rumour without inquiry,
and had written offering sincere congratulations on
his pardon, obtained through the interest of the
Prince of Wales. At every stage, sufferings seemed
to be gratuitously accumulating for him. The night
before the list of those "ordered for execution" arrived
at the gaol, he passed in a very miserable condition.
He was full of anxiety to know the result. Next
morning the "friends" came to break the news gently
to him; but with a natural instinct he stopped them, and
said he read the whole in their faces. He afterwards
told the ordinary that it was only during these last
three days that he had really been persuaded to entertain any hope—that is, from the receipt of the letter
about the Prince of Wales—but that from the very
first he had looked on himself as a lost man. On the
Sunday morning he complained, as he lay in bed, of a
pain in his side, and the ordinary asked what it came
from. He replied with something of pathos, "Lethalis
arundo! and a deadly arrow indeed!"

To the end Johnson proved himself the true
friend. As soon as the fatal warrant was signed,
he took the trouble of obtaining, through his friend
Mr. Chamier, an exact account of the disposition of

the Court, and what *real* chances there were of even a respite. This letter, which, though unfavourable, was to be depended on, he had sent to the condemned. He had worked while there was hope, and a chance of hope. Now there were but a few days left, and it was charity and true kindness to let the prisoner concentrate his thoughts on a more suitable subject.

Johnson had done all he could, but there was more required from him. It was Sunday, June the 22nd, and the terrible day, fixed for Friday, was drawing on rapidly. Johnson had gone down to Streatham, and was sitting in the Thrale pew of the little church of that place, his mind perhaps wandering away to the miserable prisoner up in London, when a letter was hurriedly brought in to him, during the service, which he read as hurriedly, and then left the church. He said afterwards, humbly, that he trusted that he should be forgiven, if he for once deserted the service of God for that of man. It would be only a Pharisee —and there was found such a Pharisee—that could bring him to task for such a dereliction.

The letter was an agitated letter, written that very morning by the miserable prisoner, and sent down by express to Johnson. It is in a tone of prostration— almost of despair. "If his Majesty," it said, piteously, "could be moved to spare me and my family the horrors and ignominy of a *public death*, which the *public* itself is solicitous to waive, and grant me in some distant, silent corner of the globe, to pass the remainder of my days in penitence and prayer, I would bless his clemency and be humbled." Johnson went home, and wrote a letter to the king—a well-written document; but, like all the rest, fatally betraying the hand that wrote, and the head that dictated. It ended in the same sentiments with which Dodd had written to Johnson, only Johnson put " to hide my guilt in some *obscure* corner of. a foreign country," instead of that, " *silent,* distant corner of the globe." After all, a simple letter from the prisoner might have been more efficacious than this vicarious entreaty. Part of it ran :

" Sir,—May it not offend your Majesty that the most miserable of men applies himself to your clemency as his last hope and last refuge from the horror and ignominy of a public execution." And he then forcibly alludes to " the spectacle of a clergyman dragged through the streets to a death of infamy, amidst the derision of the profligate and the profane." This was skilfully adapted to appeal to the royal mind.*

With this letter he sent a wholesome caution, which yet reflects his honest sympathy and goodness of heart.

"Sir,—I most seriously enjoin you not to let it be at all known that I have written this letter, and to return the copy to Mr. Allen in a cover to me. I hope I need not tell you that I wish it success. But do not indulge hope. Tell nobody."

He had interpreted truly and sagaciously the little signs of mercy.

But this true and manful ally went yet further.

* Boswell, in his incomparable Biography, has given a list of all Johnson's contributions to this unhappy case.

We know him to have been full of a rough, sturdy pride, which made him always disinclined to ask personal favours, especially where a poor chance of success would bring with it the mortification of a refusal. But he did not scruple to sacrifice all personal feelings. He actually brought himself to write an application, in his own name, and signed with the well-known "SAM. JOHNSON," to Mr. Jenkinson, then Secretary-at-War, begging his interposition—a very short letter, but a very close and admirable letter, in which he urged the topics he had put forward in the newspaper article; and it will be seen, by a single dramatic expression, how forcibly he could put it. One motive he urged was that he was "the first clergyman of our Church who has suffered public execution for immorality; and I know not whether it would not be more for the interest of religion to bury such an offender in the obscurity of perpetual exile than to *expose him in a cart*, and on the gallows, to all who, for any reason, are enemies to the clergy." This was well put, in days when the cry was, that there were many such enemies abroad. And he added to it another weighty motive. "Supreme power," he said, "has in all ages paid some attention to the voice of the people; and that voice does not least deserve to be heard when it calls out for mercy. There is now a *very general desire that Dodd's life should be spared*. More is not wished; and, perhaps, this is not too much to be granted."

He was naturally reluctant to make this personal application, but he said later, that when Dodd was on the scaffold he would say to himself, "I would not have been here, if he had written;" and then added, a little vehemently, " Sir, I could *not bear* the thought of *that*." He could not; for with that great, feeling heart, the idea of a fellow-man suffering through some moral omission of his, was indeed agony.

Mr. Jenkinson was Secretary-at-War—scarcely the proper source of mercy to apply to. That letter was never noticed. Perhaps, it was thought " an intrusion," as Johnson put it in his letter; but it does not seem likely; as Mr. Jenkinson (later becoming Lord Hawksbury) wrote in his " polite answer" to Boswell, that it never reached its destination. That noble person said, he never received it; which, however, may be read, that he never *recollected* receiving it.

It was now the very last day before the execution. In the morning he said to the ordinary, " What a dreadful day of trial was before him, as he had to go through the parting with his wife."

Mr. Thicknesse made his way in to visit him, in the stream of " friends." Justly he says, that the wretched man " suffered a thousand deaths" before he died. He found Mrs. Dodd there, delirious, and in a fever. The prisoner, himself, had not closed his eyes all night, on account of the crash of fetters being un-riveted, for the execution of some criminals in the morning. " Every blow was a shock." He had got Thicknesse to go to Lord Orwell to get his signature. But that nobleman, who was glad to have the fashionable clergyman to dinner, declined to have anything to do with him, now that the blight of

Newgate had settled on him—a truly characteristic trait.

I wonder, on this occasion, did that curious passage in his early novel occur to him, which seems an anticipation of his own fate? " The time for his execution is fixed. . . . . He applied to all those great friends . . . . and begged them to use all their interest in his favour. *One of his friends,* more especially with whom he had lived in great esteem, gave him the severest shock. In answer he received the following letter . . . . ' It surprises me, that you have the confidence to make any application to me, when you well know that I am perfectly convinced *you deserve the fate you are about to suffer.' "* Almost the answer Lord Orwell gave.

The " friends" were still exerting themselves. As the interval narrowed, the expedients grew more desperate. A thousand pounds were easily got together; and, it is said, his gaoler's fidelity was tempted with this large sum; but Mr. Akerman declined it.* During his last days, a man hung about the gaol with five hundred pounds in his pocket, seeking to gain over some of the meaner officials. But a yet more difficult plan was then laid out.

There was a Mrs. Wright in London about this time, very cunning in wax modelling, and of some reputation in that art. She told Mr. Thicknesse how she had actually modelled Dodd's head, and " carried it to him under her petticoats." The plan offered some favourable chances. The room was large and long.

* Johnson and others confirm this story.

M

There was always a stream of friends coming and going, and it did seem feasible to dress up a figure in the Doctor's clothes, place it at the table, with his "large hat flapped down over his eyes." The keeper, who would look in at the door, would be quite satisfied. But Doctor Dodd, it was said, had not the intrepidity to carry out the scheme (and it did require intrepidity); and, what is a more honourable motive for not adopting it, was afraid of compromising the generous governor, Mr. Akerman, who had shown him great indulgence, and relaxed the prison rules. But the truth was, the chances were too desperate, and an escape after the pattern of Lord Nithsdale, only thirty years before, was not to be so readily compassed. It was accordingly given up.

As I have said, a stream of friends kept pouring in and passing out, comforting, planning, talking, so that the unhappy man had small opening for the serious thought his situation required. This excitement, it is to be feared, to his very end, buoyed him up with the hopes of a reprieve—he being shut out from the world, with powerful agencies reporting to him every hour *how* they had been at work. He was shocked and overwhelmed when he was told that there was in truth no hope. But in a short time he recovered himself and behaved with calmness. Yet horrors only seemed to gather. Mrs. Dodd's sister, "Eleonora," had actually sunk under the wearing anxiety. Yet the friends continued to come and go to the very end, eager to see, to comfort, possibly to talk, certainly to disturb.* Those well-meant offices

* It suggests very forcibly the last hours of Palmer.

must have kept him in a perfect tumult, and hindered him from getting ready for the tremendous ordeal before him.

During this last day he wrote a farewell letter to his faithful Weedon Butler.

"As this is the last letter you are likely ever to receive from me, I have taken a large sheet of paper . . . Oh, pray for me, my friend, in the last dread scene! I am all weakness and imperfection! May the Lord Jesus vouchsafe to support and strengthen my feeble soul. . . . On Friday, my friend, my beloved, I shall be no more! Weep my sad fate, and with tender affection remember that you knew a man once, by God's love, the happiest that could be in His blessed service, but who, seduced by the world and sin, plunged into woe as bitter as ever was experienced on earth. Adieu! Adieu!"

It was now come to the Wednesday, and at midnight of that day, perhaps the first disengaged moment he could find, he sat down and wrote a few lines to Samuel Johnson, dated June 23, midnight.

"Accept," it ran, "thou great and good heart, my earnest and fervent thanks and prayers;" and then alludes pathetically to having sought his knowledge at an early hour in life. "I pray to God most sincerely to bless you with the highest transports, and admitted, as I trust I shall be, to the realms of bliss before you, I shall hail your arrival there with transport, and rejoice to acknowledge that you were my comforter, my advocate, and my friend. God be ever with you!"

That morning Johnson had sent him the following

letter, admirable, as it seems to me, for its brevity, for
its weight, and for its words of true comfort; and, in
truth, worth pages of the common-places which another—as well meaning, perhaps, but who did not
know the human heart so well—might have written:

"DEAR SIR,—That which is appointed to all men
is now coming upon you. Outward circumstances in
the eyes and thoughts of men are below the notice of
an immortal being about to stand the trial for eternity
before the Supreme Judge of heaven and earth. Be
comforted: your crime, morally or religiously considered, has no very deep dye of turpitude; it corrupted no man's principles; it attacked no man's life;
it involved only a temporary and reparable injury.
Of this and of all other sins you are earnestly to
repent, and may GOD, who knoweth your frailty and
desireth not our death, accept your repentance, for
the sake of his Son, JESUS CHRIST our Lord.

"In requital of these well-intended offices which
you are pleased so emphatically to acknowledge, let
me beg that you make in your devotions one petition
for my eternal welfare.

"I am, dear Sir, your affectionate servant,

"SAM. JOHNSON."

We almost hear these manly practical words. Let
us think, too, how delicately he moderated his own
strong sentiments, without at the same time any
delusive flatteries—for there was no one who thought
so awfully of the terrors of death and the tremendous
responsibilities it brought with it. There is even an

artful topic of comfort suggested in the first sentence, as though what was coming on Dodd was only a little in anticipation of what was coming on all.

There were people who had the hardihood to bring Johnson to task for the charitable close of his letter. The criminal, on receipt of it, put it into his wife's hand, and charged her never to part with it; for this was now his last day, and she was come to take leave of him.

To the very end the stream of friends kept pouring in and pouring out. To the very last, hope was kept fluttering before his eyes. Towards night, however, he took the opportunity of justifying the king and his councillors, and called his friends to witness that he did not in the least blame them for the decision that had been arrived at, and which he was sure was conceived in a spirit of justice. He then lifted up his hands and prayed for the king.

The well-meaning but intrusive Thicknesse found his way in even at this sacred moment, and describes with much natural pathos a scene of dreadful anguish—his parting with his wife. "A situation," he says, "not to be described or conceived." "I walked up to them," he goes on, "and found their hands locked in each other's, and *their minds as much departed as if they had both been dead.* Plainly perceiving that they neither saw me nor one another, I quitted the room. At that moment," he adds, "I coveted sovereign power." Others who saw the same dreadful scene, say that she could just murmur, "God give me strength to bear this!" and fainted off into a dead swoon. Going home, he wrote the Doctor a letter containing some proposals " such as no rational man would have given ;" and received this reply, which is even now almost distressing to read, and which seems actually to reflect agitation and despair :

" DEAR SIR,—I am just at present not very well, and incapable of judging. I shall communicate your kind paper to my friends. Many thanks for your attention. I rather think it would do hurt, and be deemed a mob.

" Yours in great misery,
" W. D."

Yours in great misery ! This was his last day, and yet the friends were coming and going, distracting him with plans. A terrible day. Outside, the exertions went on. Toplady, a Methodist preacher, was putting up public prayers for him ; and a Methodist woman actually got close up to the king's carriage window and poured in a volley of imprecations for his inhumanity. On this day, too, was seen a man—the man with the five hundred pounds in his pocket—skulking about the gaol trying to corrupt the gaoler ; but there was no hope. But a wild scheme for the day of execution had been thought of, and planned.

His friends stayed with him until very late, some of them comforting him with the old " common form" of comfort, that it was " a wretched world," and the like. " No, no," said the wretched prisoner, " it has been a very pleasant world to me !" " I respect

him," said Johnson, "for thus speaking the truth."
"Sir," he said later, in his forcible way, "Dodd would
have given *both his hands and both his legs to have
lived.*" He was, indeed, hungering and thirsting after
life, and it was growing sweeter to him as it was
growing shorter. Later the friends departed—the
last night of life ended for him. He went to rest—
and slept.*

* "Of all states upon earth none is so distracting as that of suspense: how dreadful are the long hours of expectation." Thus wrote
Doctor Dodd in his novel, many years before.

CHAPTER THE FIFTEENTH.

THE PROCESSION.

IT was now the morning of Friday, the 27th. When they went to call the hapless criminal, he did not at first recollect what was to take place, and presently, on its coming back upon him, suffered the most dreadful horror "and agony of mind," becoming outrageously vehement in his speech and looks; but, on leaving the chapel, his face was seen to exhibit the greatest calmness and composure.

Mr. Villette, who filled the dreadful office of "Ordinary of Newgate," attended on him, together with the chaplain of the Magdalen, Mr. Dobey. The friends who had been there the preceding night also appeared upon this occasion; and all moved on to the chapel. In the vestry they met the other criminal, who was to suffer also—Harris, the youth convicted for the "two half sovereigns and some silver," and who had attempted suicide in his cell. Him Doctor Dodd addressed with "great tenderness and emotion of heart" on the heinousness of his offence, and begged that the other clergyman might be called in to assist in moving the heart of the poor youth. But "the Doctor's words," says one who stood by, "were the most pathetic and effective." All who looked on were greatly affected, and shed tears.

Coming from the chapel, he prayed aloud for his friends; then said to some one near him: "Now, my dear friend, speculation is at an end; all must be real." It was now half-past eight, and they were waiting for the officers. He bid his friends, who were all weeping round, pray for him; to whom they said, "We pray more than language can utter."

The Doctor was now gently told that he must submit to being bound; but he looked up and said, "I feel I am free: *my* freedom will be there." In this last act, we may accept all his behaviour as natural, genuine, and untheatrical. Even the men apologised to him for their duty; but he thanked them heartily for their consideration. The miserable Harris was utterly overcome, and it was noticed that his limbs had got all distorted.

He was offered assistance as they crossed the yard, but he declined it with " seeming pleasure." " No," he said, "I am firm as a rock." Then they passed out at what was called "The Felons' Gate," through which the malefactors always left the gaol to ascend the fatal cart.

The deep bell of St. Sepulchre's had been booming out solemnly from seven o'clock. In the press-yard a crowd of respectable persons were waiting; and by nine o'clock the unhappy Doctor, with his fellow-sufferer, Harris, made his appearance. He was in deep black, and in a large full-bottomed wig. At what was called the "Little Gate of Newgate," that looked into the yard, an immense crowd was gathered of a more indiscriminate sort, from whom the turn-keys levied a shilling each for the short glimpse they were to have of the criminals. But nothing could have been more decent than their behaviour. There was not a dry eye there, but the name of the Chief Justice was said to have been often heard.

It was now a quarter past nine. From an early hour all London had been astir. Tens of thousands had come in from the country to see the spectacle. With the lower class of workmen, "hanging days," as they were coarsely called, even on common occasions, were always taken as holidays; and customers press-ing to have orders executed hurriedly, were reminded of this. Among the "bucks" of higher rank it had become a favourite sensation. Selwyn's craze is well known—a taste, too, that was shared by Thomas Warton the poet, and the Duke of Montagu, some of whom Foote, in his rude jocularity, called "The Hanging Committee." Among a less distinguished class, it was common to meet at "The Rainbow," in Bedford-row, and notably at "The Shakspeare," to make up little pleasant parties to sit up all night and go and see the "hanging" next morning. A strange, almost brutal, sensational fancy, but quite in keeping with the savage tone of manners of the time.

The hapless Doctor's last procession was about to begin. This, too, was another stage of the barbarity;

for he was to be led along slowly a distance of three miles, all through London, to Tyburn. A crowd of the sturdier ruffians waited round "The Felons' Gate" to see him ascend his carriage, and these were to be his attendants to the end; for they put their strong thews to profit, and took pride in keeping their place through the whole journey.

The Doctor was allowed to go in a mourning-coach with four horses, a favour accorded to the more respectable criminals.* Harris was placed in a cart draped with black baize. With the Doctor were Villette, the Newgate ordinary, who had seen scores of these ceremonials; Mr. Dobey, the clergyman; and Leapingwell, the sheriff's officer. After them came a hearse and four, containing a white open shell. Then it began to move. Even under a great flapped hat which he wore, his "corpse-like" appearance was noticed by many. During this time he scarcely spoke, but kept his eyes shut, trying to meditate. The chaplain was saying prayers beside him, when he broke out very naturally, that it was very hard that mankind should not be more merciful. He

---

* The Perreaus had been thus indulged, as was also Ryland the engraver a little later, and the Reverend Mr. Hackman, who shot Miss Ray. It is surprising that Boswell was not present at this execution. He had been at the Perreaus' trial and execution, and had made acquaintance with the notorious Mrs. Rudd, who had figured so conspicuously in that affair. He was at Ryland's, and had seen many convicts of a more common description at Tyburn. Shortly after Dodd's death, he actually secured a place in the mourning-coach with Hackman and the clergyman, and travelled with him all that dismal route from Newgate to Tyburn. This is a feature in Boswell not yet noted.

added presently, however, "Why should my fleshy heart repine at death?"

Can a more terrible pageant be conceived than that funeral, as it were, of the living, trailing by slowly past the Old Bailey, through Newgate-street, Snow-hill, and Holborn, and into Oxford-street—for we have the whole details of the day from one who was actually present, and who stood in Mr. Langdale the distiller's window, with Abel and Bach the musicians, and saw it go by.

All along that three miles the whole of London was out in the streets, waiting and expectant. The authorities were scared by the popular feeling, and two thousand men were kept drawn up in Hyde Park, ready for an emergency. Every window was open up to the roof, and eager faces filled every window, look-ing out. There was a fever of expectation and a roar of voices. Then the crowds were seen coming —specially the strong ruffians, who had begun their march at "The Felons' Gate," heading the dismal progress, and gathering as they came; and the lugubrious mourning-coach moving along slowly; and the cart behind it, on which was the other criminal. As it passed, a glimpse was seen of the wretched Doctor within, whose face, of a "ghastly and sepulchral" paleness, struck every spectator. People in the windows sobbed aloud. But the strangest effect is described to have been, when, with a decorous respect, ten thousand hats were swept from ten thousand heads; and the strange, chameleon-like change of the seething, floating mass from darkness to light and whiteness, struck one who was looking down from above. What contributed, too, to the tragic effect, was the father of the other convict, who sat on the cart and supported his son's head on his lap, and whose grey hairs and streaming eyes moved every heart, and, it is said, even diverted sympathy from the leading sufferer.

Opposite St. Sepulchre's they stopped, according to old custom, to hear some solemn words from "the Bellman"—exactly as William Griffith, the highwayman whom Doctor Dodd had convicted, had stopped not long before.

Here the miserable Harris quite fainted away, so that water had to be brought to recover him. "The Bellman" then did his office, of which the other seemed quite insensible, and his cart moved on to give place to the mourning-coach, and to the wretched Doctor at its window. Nothing more touching or more effectual can be conceived for producing a fitting tone in the crowd, or even in the criminal, than this exhortation. This also was devised by the charity of Master Robert Dowe. "The Bellman," stepping forward and ringing his bell, thus addressed the unhappy Doctor:

"All good people, pray heartily unto God for these poor sinners, who are now going to their death, for whom this great bell doth toll.

"You that are condemned to die repent with lamentable tears; ask mercy of the Lord for the salvation of your souls though the merits, death, and passion of Jesus Christ, who now sits at the right hand of God, to make intercession for as many of you as penitently return unto Him.

"Lord have mercy upon you! Christ have mercy upon you! Lord have mercy upon you! Christ have mercy upon you!"

When he came to the close of this touching appeal, "Lord have mercy upon you!" Doctor Dodd wrung his hands bitterly. With a strange want of decency, the old churchyard had been built up with wooden stands, and was blackened over with human figures, who looked on at this dismal spectacle.

Then they moved on again. At St. Giles's the block became tremendous, and they had to stop often. It must have been an agonising pilgrimage for the chief actor, whose "corpse-like face," says one who saw it, was framed, as it were, in the mourning-coach window. No wonder he said that he would gladly have died in the prison yard. He prayed all the way. They had actually to pass by his former house—the one in Pall-Mall, where he took in his genteel pupils—and it affected him greatly. At last it all ended, and they were now at Tyburn.

Johnson had written an address for him, a sort of contrite confession, which was to have been read at the gallows; but, owing to the enormous crowds, who would not have heard a word of it, it was wisely and decorously omitted.

They were more than two hours reaching the place, and the scene there was yet more exciting.

CHAPTER THE SIXTEENTH.

TYBURN.

FROM eight o'clock it had been crowded. All
the house-tops that commanded a view were covered.
The windows were filled. The trees—and there
were many trees then in Tyburnia—were literally
loaded with human beings. Huge galleries—erected
by a notorious speculator, the wife of a cow-
keeper, and known popularly as "Mother Proctor's
Pews"—grew up the day before, like a stand at a
race-course, and furnished an excellent view of the
dismal show. Places here brought high prices, and
it was said that at Earl Ferrers's execution over five
hundred pounds had been cleared by the "Tyburn
Boxes." Others, of humbler degree, paid a shilling for
standing room on a cart.

In Hogarth's plate of the Idle Apprentice's execution
we have the whole scene—the mourning-coach, with
the chaplain's face in the window; the loaded trees,
and the open country, where fashionable streets now

cluster thickly; and even Mother Proctor's Boxes, built of rude timber, with men at the top letting off pigeons. Here are the women and their babies, the ballad-singers selling the "Last Dying Speech," printed the day before; and the cart, shaped like a two-wheeled Pickford's van, with the officers in front.

On the top of an unfinished house close by were seen Charles Fox and the Abbé Raynal.* There was much impatience, as the procession was delayed. Just before it arrived—as if to throw an air of burlesque over the unhappy prisoner's sufferings—a sow got into the enclosed space, and was baited after the usual fashion, its distress causing roars of laughter in the crowd.

At last, the head of the procession came in sight. From the loaded trees, from the carts, from the Tyburn Boxes, the roar of voices and excitement became tremendous. Sheriff Thomas led the way, and after him the City marshals and mounted constables; then the mourning-coaches slowly debouched.

Selwyn, that notorious amateur, was, strange to say, not present; but he had friends who knew his taste, and who furnished the fullest details. Storer, one of the wild, unprincipled set who were his friends, had a good place, and observed everything.† To this *blasé* man of fashion, who thought the whole

---

* See " Love and Madness," p. 102. Sir Herbert Croft, the author gives his honour for this fact.

† This taste of Selwyn's, for which a " morbid fancy" is too lenient a term, was questioned seriously some years ago, but has been perfectly well established.

performance very insipid, we owe a sort of photograph of the proceedings.

The weather had been variable all the morning, a strong wind being abroad, with heavy showers coming on every now and then. The ghastly ceremonial then began. Harris was speedily despatched; then the mourning-coach drew up closer, and the Doctor descended.

Every eye was turned on that ghastly face, seen under the heavy broad-brimmed hat, "flapped down" so closely all over his face. Mr. Storer was quite near, and said he seemed stupid from despair; but a constable, a better judge in such matters, who told the whole story to Lord March, said he never saw a man behave better.* It was told, also, how earnestly he prayed; but, adds this fashionable scoffer, who was writing at Almack's, and in a hurry to get to Ranelagh, "*that* was in his profession."

As he appeared on the fatal cart a heavy shower came down. Under the great flapped hat his eyes were never lifted, and the corpse-like face was turned to the ground. He was heard praying aloud for his wretched self and for his more wretched wife. The clergymen prayed with him; but it was noted how one, Mr. Dobey, was deeply affected, while the other, Villette, hardened to his office, was "perfectly indifferent and unfeeling in everything he said and

---

* Several spectators—besides the reporters of newspapers—have left accounts of what they saw. Storer was in the "Tyburn Boxes;" Angelo, the fencing-master, at Mr. Langdale's, the distiller's; and Archenholtz, a Prussian traveller, was at Tyburn. They all agree wonderfully.

N

did." * There seems to have been no limit to the indulgence of time, and this praying, and instructions, and preparation, went on for nearly an hour; so that the people grew very impatient, and were eager for what they had come to see, to begin.

The executioner now drew near, and put the rope about his neck, which he himself assisted in adjusting; but he still kept on his broad flapped hat and wig. Suddenly a gust came and blew it off, and a murmur went round as the corpse-like face was exposed to a full gaze. He was a little embarrassed, but resumed his praying when it was restored to him. Another spectator remarked the almost piteous burlesque in the fitting on of the nightcap. Even the tenderest, it was said, could not but be sensible of this impression.†

Now at last the moment was come, and the unhappy man was making his final preparations. Even at this awful moment everything seemed to go wrong. He took off his great hat, and with it came his wig, which the executioner gave him back, and which he put on ‡ and took off again. He then took

* Archenholtz, who was a stranger, tells a story of this heartlessness of the ordinary. Villette worked his experiences of Dodd's last moments into a pamphlet (on every copy of which he wrote his name), which was sold enormously for his own benefit. But a more significant act of his, was the publication, only a year before, of the *Newgate Calendar*, with "virtuous" and "improving" reflections attached. (See Appendix VII.)

† Sir Herbert Croft. Though this account is thrown into the form of a novel, the details may be accepted as accurate. "Every guinea in my pocket," says the writer, "would I have given that he had not worn a wig; or that, wearing one, the cap had been bigger."

‡ "Why he put on his wig again," wrote Storer, "I know not."

out a cap, and tried to fit it on, but found it too
small, and had to get aid. The truth was, the poor
wretch scarcely knew what he was doing. A sort of
ghastly smile was seen on his face as it was fitted to
his head. He prayed with extraordinary intensity,
and took leave of his friends. Just before he drew
the cap down on his face he gave money to the executioner, and it was remembered afterwards that he had
whispered him very earnestly. This was thought
to be an injunction to put him out of pain speedily,
by hanging on his legs, and thus shorten the struggle.
But the hurried instructions were in a very different
spirit. Even now, at the end, a dismal, ghastly will-
o'-the-wisp of a hope was to flutter over his dying
agony, and he was to die with a faint and horrible
possibility that after all he might be saved. For the
hangman had been gained by a large bribe, and he
had adjusted the rope in some way by which it was
believed it would not press so much on the throat;
and the Doctor had been cautioned not to stir or
struggle if he could help it.

The cart now moved away. For a second there
was an awful silence. Then there was heard a sort
of prolonged gasp, or hissing, as of air drawn in
between many teeth.* There was heard the sharp,

The quiet and perfectly genuine manner in which the London rake
writes of the whole business, as a sort of bore which he was enduring
for the sake of his friend, is truly characteristic. "I stayed till he
was cut down: and could not conceive an execution with so few inci
dents." Lord March intended going, but was too late; "though I
believe," he adds, "from what I have heard, the Doctor would have
been very glad to have waited for me." This wild company had their
jest at everything.

* "This was done so universally at the fatal moment, that I am

sudden scream of a woman, as the dark figure swung
in the air. At such a moment how was he to think
of those last private instructions or avoid struggling.
After about two minutes all was over, and the hapless
man hung motionless.

But this was not to be the end. A sort of ghastly
mystery was destined to wait on the end of another
gay clergyman—Laurence Sterne, who lived gaily
and died miserably, and even after death was dragged
from his grave by resurrection-men and sold for
dissection. For Doctor Dodd, as clerical, as gay
and almost as fashionable as Yorick, was to begin
another mystery. The indefatigable "friends" had
been busy to the end, and had hope even after the
end.

Everything had been arranged. At Mr. Davies's,
an undertaker in Goodge-street, a warm bath was
kept ready, and there also was waiting John Hunter,
the famous surgeon, who had just been attracting
notice for some remarkable experiments for restoring
the drowned to life.* Mr. Hawes, the founder of
the Humane Society, who had before exerted himself for Dodd, seems to have originated this idea.
Long after wild stories went about as to the means

persuaded the noise might have been heard at a considerable distance.
For my own part, I detected myself, in a certain manner, accompany-
ing his body with a motion of my own; as you have seen people
wreathing, and twisting, and biassing themselves, after a bowl which
they have just delivered."—*Love and Madness.*

* The whole of this account is vouched for by Hutton, the mathe-
matician, who heard Hunter tell it at a sort of club held at Slaughter's
Coffee-house, of which Doctor Banks and Doctor Solander, and other
men of science, were members.—*See Newcastle Magazine,* vol. i. p. 18.

that had been employed to give success to the attempt. It was said that a heavy weight had been sewn up in his clothes, to which a small cord was attached, so as by some means to keep the pressure off the neck.* And it is perfectly certain that instructions were given that his legs were not to be pulled.

Nor was there anything so wild in the idea of success. The pleasant Doctor Glover had earned a sort of celebrity in Dublin by restoring to life a criminal who had been hanged; but who repaid the service by persecuting his preserver for money, alleging that the hand that had given him life was bound to preserve it.† But what may have suggested the idea more directly was a more remarkable instance which was seen in the Irish papers, among the circuit news—mentioned almost as a thing of course—where a man had been hung at Carlow, and being cut down after the usual time, had come back to consciousness. With the barbarity of the day, he was kept a month, brought out, and hung once more!

After hanging the usual time, the body was cut down, and given over to his friends, who had a mourning-coach waiting.‡ But the crowd was so enormous and so excited, and their curiosity so vehement, that it was found impossible almost to get to the coach. Even then the passage was blocked. Thus precious minutes, and even precious hours, were lost. The undertaker's house was far away;

---

* *Newcastle Magazine,* vol. i. p. 18.
† Taylor, Recollections, i. 219.
‡ It was only in cases of murder that the body was *not* given up.

and when, at last, John Hunter was reached, it seemed quite hopeless. He worked long and perseveringly, but fruitlessly. In the unhappy Doctor's case everything was to fail.*

But the story of the attempt at restoration got abroad, even on the next day; and a firm persuasion seized on many minds, which was kept alive long after, that the Doctor had been seen in foreign countries. By one account he had been at Dunkirk; and a few years later, an Aberdeen paper published a letter from Provence, dated July 12, 1777, which described the Doctor as living there happily, "and beyond the reach of his enemies." †

Complaints were made of his body being smuggled away for private burial, whereas the Perreaus were interred openly. This sort of suspicion was the only foundation for such rumours. The unhappy Doctor was indeed dead; and it is only to be lamented that the last moments of such a life should have been disturbed by such a vain *ignis fatuus*, the very ghost of a hope.

That night his faithful friend Weedon Butler had him carried away down to Cowley, in Middlesex, where he was buried with quick lime in the coffin, at the north side of the church; where, too, the faithful Butler came often afterwards, and wept over his unhappy friend's grave. An inscription, the baldest

---

* The real difficulty in these cases of suspended animation lies in this: from the absence of air, the blood gets *corrupted*, and the substance of the brain injured. The popular belief is, that the mere strangulation and stoppage of air to the lungs causes death.

† *Newcastle Magazine.*

and simplest that could be given, was placed over it, without the usual "Hic jacet:"

REV. WILLIAM DODD,

BORN MARCH 29, 1729;

DIED JUNE 27, 1777,

IN THE 49TH YEAR OF HIS AGE.

The clerk of his Bedford Chapel, who was present during the attempts at resuscitation, took a cast of the head, and made several plaster busts, which were considered excellent likenesses. And on the Sunday after the Doctor's execution, the same person invited attention to the suit of black he wore, which he assured a gentleman, was the very one in which the Doctor died.

The hapless wife never held up her head again. The verger's daughter—so tolerant, so enduring, so faithful to the end—dragged on a hopeless life at Ilford, in Essex, "in circumstances of corporal and mental inanity," says one who knew her and relieved her wants, until the year 1784, when she died. A short paragraph in the papers mentioned the fact, and reminded the public that she was the relict of the "unfortunate Doctor Dodd," who had "suffered at Tyburn a few years before."

Which ends the history of this curious tragedy. There is no need to sum up his character. That can be gathered sufficiently from the story that has just been told. Or may we accept the bitter etching given in Walpole's Journal, and which, as Doctor Doran has remarked, is not overdone:

"He was, undoubtedly, a bad man, who employed religion to promote his ambition; humanity to establish a character, and, it is to be hoped, to indulge his good-natured sensations; and any means to gratify his passions or vanity, and to extricate himself out of their distressing consequences. Not a professed Methodist; but his vices, pleasures, fondness for dress and luxury being less under command than the hypocritical self-denial of those more artful impostors, and his thirst for preferment being more impetuous than their patient appetite for solid power, he made use of their credit as a party, rather than attached himself to their party." A life, too, from which we could draw a moral—either in one of the suspicious common-places with which the Ordinary of Newgate wound up the written lives of his malefactors, " Thus, then, we see, how," &c.; or more effectually in Dodd's own words taken from his questionable novel: "Ye sons of lawless pleasure contemplate and be abashed, boast no more of your speedy palling joys; but to obtain happiness, sure and lasting, scorn the delusions of flattering iniquity, and live under the protection of real honour and firm integrity."

APPENDIX.

APPENDIX.

———•———

I.

EXTRACT FROM VILLETTE'S ACCOUNT.

" On the morning of his death I went to him, with the Reverend Mr. Dobey, chaplain of the Magdalen, whom he had desired to attend him to the place of execution. He appeared composed; and when I asked him how he had been supported, he said he had had some comfortable sleep, by which he should be the better enabled to perform his duty.

" As we went from his room, in our way to the chapel, we were joined by his friends, who had spent the foregoing evening with him, and also by another clergyman. When we were in the vestry adjoining the chapel, he exhorted his fellow-sufferer, who had attempted to destroy himself, but had been prevented by the vigilance of the keeper. He spoke to him with great tenderness and emotion of heart, entreating him to consider that he had but a short time to live, and that it was highly necessary that he, as well as himself, made good use of their time, implored pardon of God under a deep sense of sin, and looked to that Lord by whose mercy alone sinners could be saved. He desired me to call in the other gentleman, who likewise assisted him to move the heart of the poor youth: but the Doctor's words were the most pathetic and effectual. He lifted up his hands, and cried out, 'O Lord Jesus, have mercy on us, and give, O give unto him, my fellow-sinner, that as we suffer together, we may go together to Heaven!' His conversation to this poor youth was so moving, that tears flowed from the eyes of all present.

"When we went into the chapel to prayer and the holy communion, true contrition and warmth of devotion appeared evident in him throughout the whole service. After it was ended, he again addressed himself to Harris in the most moving and persuasive manner, and not without effect: for he declared that he was glad he had not made away with himself, and said he was easier, and hoped he should now go to heaven. The Doctor told him how Christ had suffered for them; and that he himself was a greater sinner than he, as he had sinned more against light and conviction, and therefore his guilt was greater; and that, as he was confident that mercy was shown to his soul, so he should look to Christ, and trust in His merits.

"He prayed God to bless his friends who were present with him, and to give his blessing to all his brethren the clergy; that he would pour out his spirit upon them, and make them true ministers of Jesus Christ, and that they might follow the divine precepts of their heavenly Master. Turning to one who stood near him, he stretched out his hand, and said, 'Now, my dear friend, speculation is at an end; all must be real! what poor, ignorant beings we are!' He prayed for the Magdalens, and wished they were there, to sing for him the 23rd Psalm.

"After he had waited some time for the officers, he asked what o'clock it was? and being told that it was half an hour after eight, he said, 'I wish they were ready, for I long to be gone.' He requested of his friends, who were in tears about him, to pray for him: to which he was answered by two of them. 'We pray more than language can utter.' He replied, 'I believe it.'

"At length he was summoned to go down into a part of the yard which is enclosed from the rest of the gaol, where the two unhappy convicts and the friends of the Doctor were alone. On his seeing two prisoners looking out of the windows, he went to them, and exhorted them so pathetically, that they both wept abundantly. He said once, 'I am now a spectacle to men, and shall soon be a spectacle to angels.'

"Just before the sheriff's officers came with the halters, one who was walking with him told him that there was yet a little solemnity he must pass through before he went out. He asked, 'What is that?' 'You will be bound.' He looked up, and said, 'Yet I am free; my freedom is there,' pointing upwards. He bore it with Christian patience, and beyond what might have been expected; and when the men offered to excuse tying his hands, he desired them to do their duty, and thanked them for their kindness. After he was bound, I offered to assist him with my arm in conducting him through the yard, where several people were assembled to see him; but he replied with seeming pleasure, 'No! I am as firm as a rock.'—As he passed along the yard, the spectators and prisoners wept and bemoaned him; and he in return, prayed God to bless them.

" On the way to execution he consoled himself in reflecting and speaking on what Christ had suffered for him; lamenting the depravity of human nature, which made sanguinary laws necessary; and said he could gladly have died in the prison yard, as being led out to public execution tended greatly to distress him. He desired me to read to him the 51st Psalm, and also pointed out an admirable penitential prayer from Rossel's Prisoner's Director. He prayed again for the king, and likewise for the people.

" When he came near the street where he formerly dwelt, he was much affected, and wept. He said, probably his tears would seem to be the effect of cowardice, but it was a weakness he could not well help; and added, he hoped he was going to a better home.

" When he arrived at the gallows, he ascended the cart, and spoke to his fellow-sufferer. He then prayed, not only for himself, but also for his wife, and the unfortunate youth that suffered with him; and declared that he died in the true faith of the gospel of Christ, in perfect love and charity with all mankind, and with thankfulness to his friends, he was launched into eternity, imploring mercy for his soul for the sake of the blessed Redeemer."

II.

The following Paper was intended to have been read by Mr. VILLETTE *at the Place of Execution, but was omitted, as it seemed not possible to communicate the knowledge of it to so great a number of persons as were then assembled.*

"To the words of dying men regard has always been paid. I am brought here to suffer death for an act of fraud, of which I confess myself guilty, with shame, such as my former state of life naturally produces, and I hope with such sorrow as He, to whom the heart is known, will not disregard. I repent that I have violated the laws by which peace and confidence are established among men; I repent that I have attempted to injure my fellow-creatures; and I repent that I have brought disgrace upon my order, and discredit upon my religion: but my offences against God are without any name or number, and can admit only of general confession and general repentance. Grant, Almighty God, for the sake of Jesus Christ, that my repentance, however late, however imperfect, may not be in vain!

"The little good that now remains in my power, is to warn others against those temptations by which I have been seduced. I have always sinned against conviction; my principles have never been shaken; I have always considered the Christian religion as a revelation from God, and its divine Author as the Saviour of the world: but the laws of God, though never disowned by me, have often been forgotten. I was led astray from religious strictness by the delusion of show and the delights of voluptuousness. I never knew or attended to the calls of frugality, or the needful minuteness of painful economy. Vanity and pleasure, into which I plunged, required expense disproportionate to my income; expense brought distress upon me; and distress, importunate distress, urged me to temporary fraud.

"For this fraud I am to die; and I die declaring, in the most solemn manner, that however I have deviated from my own precepts, I have taught others, to the best of my knowledge, and with all sincerity, the true way to eternal happiness. My life, for some few unhappy years past, has been dreadfully erroneous; *but my ministry has been always sincere.* I have constantly believed, and I now leave the world solemnly avowing my conviction, that there is no other name under heaven by which we can be saved, but only the name of the Lord Jesus; and I entreat all who are here to join me in my last petition, that for the sake of that Lord Jesus Christ, my sins may be forgiven, and my soul received into his everlasting kingdom.

" WILLIAM DODD.

" June. 27, 1777."

III.

*** In a postscript to a friend, the author writes thus :

" I forgot to request my good friend to tell Mr. Hanway, that in one of my little melancholy poems, written in this dreary place, I have made such mention of him as I think his attention to the improvement of gaols demands : that I earnestly press him, as a Christian and a man, to pursue that improvement with zeal ; that much, very much is to be done ; and that while the state of prisons remains as it is, the legislature has some reason to charge itself with the greater part of the robberies, &c., committed. For the offenders for petty crimes are here hardened in almost every species of vice ; and turned out, necessary plunderers of the public, from the depravity of their unaltered disposition, and the deficiency of proper employment. I have felt much on this subject since I have been here, and expressed something of it in the poem. Week the Third."

PIECES FOUND AMONGST THE AUTHOR'S PAPERS IN PRISON. WITH HIS LAST PRAYER.

I.

THE ADMONITION.

Afflicted prisoner, whosoe'er thou art,
  To this lone room unhappily confined ;
Be thy first business here to search thy heart,
  And probe the deep corruptions of thy mind !

o

Struck with the foul transgressions thou hast wrought,
    With sin—the source of all thy worldly woe;
To shame, to sorrow, to conviction brought,
    Oh, fall before the throne of mercy low!

With true repentance pour thy soul in prayer,
    And fervent plead the Saviour's cleansing blood:
Faith's ardent cry will pierce the Father's ear,
    And Christ's a plea which cannot be withstood!

II.

REFLECTIONS (UNFINISHED).

Here, secluse from worldly pleasure,
    In this doleful place confin'd,
Come, and let's improve the leisure,
    Meditate, my thoughtful mind!

Soul alike and body sharing,
    How have I the one forgot!
While for t'other only caring,
    Lo! my miserable lot!

Yet the one I so much cherish,
    Doom'd to death when giv'n to life,
Soon, perhaps, must sink and perish,
    Dust to dust—must end the strife!

From a tedious tour returning,
    Into distant foreign land,
How my anxious heart is burning
    News of *home* to understand!

*   *   *   *   *

IV.

HIS LAST PRAYER:

Written June 27, in the night previous to his suffering.

GREAT and glorious Lord God! Thou Father of mercies, and God of all comfort! a poor and humble *publican* stands trembling in Thy awful presence; and under the deep sense of innumerable transgressions, scarce dares so much as to lift up his eyes, or to say, *Lord, be merciful to me, a sinner!*

For I have sinned, oh Lord! I have most grievously sinned against Thee; sinned against light, against conviction; and by a thousand, thousand offences, justly provoked Thy wrath and indignation! My sins are peculiarly aggravated, and their burden more than ordinarily oppressive to my soul, from the sight and sense I have had of Thy love, and from the high and solemn obligations of my *sacred character!*

But, oppressed with consciousness, and broken in heart under the sense of guilt, I come, oh Lord! with earnest prayers and tears, supplicating Thee of Thy mercy, to look upon me; and forgive me for *His* precious merits' sake, which are infinitely more unbounded than even all the sins of a whole sinful world! By His cross and passion I implore Thee, to *spare* and to *deliver me, O Lord!*

Blessed be thy unspeakable goodness, for that wonderful display of divine love, on which alone is my hope and my confidence! Thou hast invited, oh blessed Redeemer! the burdened and heavy-laden, the sick in soul, and wearied with sin, to *come to Thee,* and *receive rest.* Lord, *I come!* Be it unto me according to Thy infallible word! Grant me Thy precious, thy inestimable REST!

Be with me, thou all-sufficient God, in the dreadful trial through which I am to pass! and graciously vouchsafe to fulfil in me those *precious promises,* which Thou, in such fatherly kindness, hast delivered to Thy afflicted children! Enable me to see and adore Thy disposing hand, in this awful, but mournful event; and to contemplate at an humble distance Thy great example; who didst go forth, bearing Thy cross, and enduring its shame, under the consolatory assurance of *the joy set before Thee!*

And oh, my triumphant Lord! in the moment of death, and in the last hour of conflict, suffer me not to want Thine especial aid! Suffer me not to doubt or despond! But sustain me in Thy arms of love; and oh receive and present faultless to Thy Father, in the robe of Thy righteousness, my poor and unworthy soul, which Thou hast redeemed with Thy most precious blood!

Thus commending myself and my eternal concerns into Thy most faithful hands, in firm hope of a happy reception into Thy kingdom; oh my God, hear me, while I humbly extend my supplications for others; and pray, that Thou wouldst bless the king and all his family; that Thou wouldst preserve the crown in his house to endless generations; and make him the happy minister of *truth,* of *peace,* and of *prosperity* to his people! Bless that *people,* oh Lord! and shine, as Thou hast done, with the light of Thy favour on this

little portion of Thy boundless creation. Diffuse more
and more a spirit of Christian piety amongst all ranks
and orders of men ; and in particular fill their hearts
with universal and undissembled love—love to Thee,
and love to each other !

Amidst the manifold mercies and blessings vouch-
safed through Thy gracious influence, Thou Sovereign Ruler of all hearts ! to so unworthy a worm,
during this dark day of my sorrows: enable me to
be thankful; and in the sincerity of heartfelt gratitude to implore Thine especial blessing on all my
beloved *fellow-creatures,* who have by any means in-
terested themselves in my preservation ! May the
prayers they have offered for me return in mercies on
their own heads ! May the sympathy they have
shown refresh and comfort their own hearts ! And
may all their good endeavours and kindnesses be
amply repaid by a full supply of Thy grace, and
abundant assistance to them in their day of distress—
in their most anxious hours of need !

To the more particular and immediate instruments
of Thy providential love and goodness to me, oh
vouchsafe to impart, Author of all good ! a rich supply
of Thy choicest comforts ! Fill their hearts with Thy
love, and their lives with Thy favour ! Guard them
in every danger: soothe them in every sorrow : bless
them in every laudable undertaking: restore an hun-
dredfold all their temporal supplies to me and mine,
and, after a course of extensive utility, advance them,
through the merits of Jesus, to lives of eternal bliss.

Extend, great Father of the world ! Thy more
especial care and kindness to my nearer and most

dear connexions. Bless with Thy continual presence and protection my dear *brother* and *sister*, and all their children and friends! hold them in Thy hand of tender care and mercy; and give them to experience that in Thee there is infinite loving-kindness and truth! Look with a tender eye on all their temporal concerns; and after lives of faithfulness and truth, oh bear them to Thy bosom, and unite us together in Thy eternal love!

But oh, my adorable Lord and Hope! suffer me in a more particular manner to offer up to Thy sovereign and gracious care my long-tried and most affectionate wife! Husband of the *widow*, be Thou her support! Sustain and console her afflicted mind! Enable her with patient submission to receive all Thy will :—and when, in Thy good time, Thou hast perfected her for Thy blessed kingdom, unite again our happy and immortal spirits in celestial love, as Thou hast been pleased to unite us in sincere earthly affection! Lord Jesus, vouchsafe unto her Thy peculiar grace and all-sufficient consolation!

If I have *any enemies*, oh Thou who *diest* for Thy enemies, hear my prayers for them! Forgive them all their ill will to me, and fill their hearts with Thy love! And, oh, vouchsafe abundantly to bless and to save all those who have either wished or done me evil! Forgive *me*, gracious God, the wrong or injury I have done to others; and *so* forgive me *my* trespasses as I freely and fully forgive all those who have in any degree trespassed against me. I desire Thy grace to purify my soul from every taint of malevolence, and to fit me, by perfect love, for the society of spirits, whose business and happiness is love!

Glory be to Thee, oh God! for all the blessings Thou hast granted me from the day of my creation until the present hour! I feel and adore Thy exceeding goodness in all: and in this *last* and *closing affliction* of my life, I acknowledge most humbly the justice of Thy fatherly correction, and bow my head with thankfulness for Thy rod! Great and good in all! I adore and magnify Thy mercy: I behold in *all* Thy love manifestly displayed; and rejoice that I am at once Thy *creature* and Thy *redeemed!*

As such, oh Lord, my *Creator* and *Redeemer*, I commit my soul into Thy faithful hands! Wash it and purify it in the blood of Thy Son from every defiling stain; perfect what is wanting in it: and grant me, poor returning, weeping, wretched prodigal—grant me the lowest place in Thy heavenly house; in and for His sole and all-sufficient merits—the adorable *Jesus;* who, with the Father and the Holy Ghost, liveth and reigneth ever one God, world without end.

Amen and amen, Lord Jesus!

V.

Dodd was a surprisingly voluminous writer. The list in "Watts's Bibliotheca" is a wonderful testimony to his industry. It should be supplemented, however, by some additional titles given in the

Gentleman's Magazine for 1777. Nicholls speaks of some quarto MS. sermons as existing a few years ago.

VI.

Johnson's industry for his wretched client was marvellous. His letter to Lord Mansfield, of which Archenholtz somehow obtained a copy, will be read with interest:

"My Lord,—But a few days—and the lot of the most unhappy of created beings will be decided for ever! I know the weight of your lordship's opinion. It is that which will undoubtedly decide, whether I am to die an ignominious death, or drag out the rest of my life in dishonourable banishment. O my Lord! do not refuse to hear what I in my humility dare to oppose to the severity of the laws.

"I feel how frightful my crime is; the sentence which condemns me is but too just: I however flatter myself, that, amidst all the reproaches cast against me on account of my crime, it will still be remembered how useful my charitable endeavours have been to that very society which I have injured. I ask for nothing but the preservation of my life, a life which I shall drag out in dishonour and perhaps in misery! Have compassion, my lord, on a man covered with infamy, without fortune, and without resource, but not, however, without fear at casting his eyes towards the abyss of eternity!

" However great that misery which will be my lot,
yet still allow me to live. That very misery under
which I shall languish the rest of my days, will fore-
warn all those who were witnesses of it, to beware of
indulging their passions, and to guard against a fatal
vanity and a spirit of dissipation.

" For the last time, I conjure you, my lord, to
suffer me to live ; and when you see me passing from
the frightful dungeon which now encloses me, to an
ignominious exile, be assured that justice will be sufficiently satisfied by the sufferings of him who is,

"My Lord,

" Your Lordship's most humble suppliant,

"WILLIAM DODD.

" Newgate, June 11, 1777."

VII.

Allusion has been made in the text to the behaviour
of Villette, the Ordinary of Newgate. The following
curious story is told by Archenholtz :

As my sole intention in recounting these transactions
is to give, by an authentic recital of facts, a just
idea of the present state of the laws of England,
and the mode of putting them in execution, I will
here recite an event that happened in London in the
year 1778, and of which, to my great astonishment, I
myself was a witness.

A young man of twenty years of age was condemned to death on the evidence of a highwayman,
who accused him of being an accomplice. His own

bad character and the testimony of the robber, accompanied with all the requisite proofs, seemed to leave no doubt of his guilt. The unhappy wretch was in consequence of this conducted in a cart to Tyburn, with some other criminals. He remained with the rope about his neck, according to the permission which the law allows, one whole hour at the foot of the gibbet. During that hour the culprit is permitted to say whatever he chooses; were he to utter high treason against the sovereign, or inflame the people to a revolt, it would be illegal to prevent him. They think humanity requires that such an alleviation should be permitted to one who is about to be launched out of the world by a violent death. There are actually a great many men, who on this sad occasion experience a certain pleasure in communicating those sentiments with which they are affected. Lord Lovat, who after the rebellion in Scotland perished on a scaffold, made use of this privilege. He declared that George II. had no right to the crown, which belonged to the Pretender alone; and added, it was with great pleasure that he was then about to shed his blood for the lawful sovereign.

The young man whom I have just mentioned said not a word, but trembling with fear, sat expectant of the awful period which was to put an end to his existence. The fatal moment at last arrives, and everything is prepared; when his accuser, turning towards Villette, the chaplain of Newgate, who is obliged to accompany the criminals to Tyburn, declares in the most solemn manner that the poor young man was innocent; and that he had been led away by the spirit of revenge to fabricate a story on purpose to procure his death. This declaration made all the spectators tremble; but the ordinary, who was accustomed to these kind of scenes, answered coldly, that it was now too late to retract. In the mean time, the people began to murmur, and some respectable persons addressed themselves to the under-sheriff, who officiated in the absence of his principal.

He having heard nothing of the confession, was about to give the fatal signal; the conductor of the cart had his whip uplifted in the air, and the cries and prayers of the unhappy wretch were still sounding in the ears of the assistants, when all on a sudden somebody cried, Halt! It was then represented to the under-sheriff how barbarous it would be to allow an innocent man to perish. The emotions of this gentleman was equally great with his astonishment; for this was a case entirely new, and without any precedent. Everybody was of opinion, that this young man ought not to be executed with the others: the cruel Villette alone insisted that he could not be saved, as the laws do not give to the officer the power of suspending the execution for a quarter of an hour. The sub-sheriff, who was acquainted with the laws, and fully convinced of the justice of Villette's observations, was now about to perform his duty with an aching heart. He had almost given the fatal order, when the high-constable addresses him as follows: "In the name of God, sir, is it possible that you can give your consent to the death of this guiltless person!" "What can I, what shall I do?" replied he. "If you will delay the execution, I will instantly mount my horse and go to the king." He accordingly departs, without hearing the cruel pleasantries of the ordinary, who prognosticated that the journey would be unsuccessful.

Four other persons were joined in the sentimental embassy, who make towards Westminster in full gallop. Tyburn is distant from St. James's two English miles. They soon arrive at the palace; but the king was gone to Richmond, and all the ministers were gone to the country, it being then the height of summer.

They then instantly repair to the offices of the secretaries of state, hoping to find some person there of whom they could receive advice; but all the clerks shrugged up their shoulders, saying, that the officer himself ought to know the extent of those powers which the law gave him. On this they return after an absence of an hour and a half, and relate the event of their unfortunate journey.

The execution of the other criminals had been suspended during this period, and Villette now insisted on the under-sheriff's giving the signal; menacing him at the same time with a criminal process, and affirming that, if he did not execute the culprit, the gaoler of Newgate would not receive him back after he had been delivered over to the executioner. The high-constable, on the other hand, asserted the contrary, and did not cease to address him with the most masculine and persuasive eloquence, until he agreed to his request. The eight other criminals were immediately hanged; and the young man, who had fainted with excessive joy, was carried back to Newgate.

The king, being informed of this event, extended his clemency that very evening to the prisoner, who, after having been conducted to the foot of the gibbet, found himself in a few hours free and happy. His Majesty also granted a pardon to the under-sheriff for having arrogated a power which he did not possess, and he received the praises of the whole nation for his boldness and humanity. To him might be applied the following line from Shakspeare:

To do a great right, he did a little wrong.

They have not in England a set of men who can properly be styled executioners. The hangman is a person employed by the sheriff; and he might gain his livelihood by any other occupation, for infamy is not there attached to his employment. It is contemptible, indeed, but it is not dishonourable; and this contempt is not attached to the action of hanging, but to the idea of its proceeding from a sordid desire of gain; for, if he could procure no other person, the sheriff would be obliged to perform the duty himself. Of this there was an instance some years since, not indeed in London, but in the country. The two men appointed for this purpose happened to die, almost at the very moment when they were about to execute their office; and the sheriff, not being able to procure any other, nor daring to delay the day or even the hour of execution, was obliged to put the criminal to death with his own hands.

The nobility in certain cases have the privileges of being beheaded: murderers, however, such as Lord Ferrers, are denied this favour. A butcher, who by his trade is best qualified for this operation, is generally employed. The family of the culprit employ him, and for this purpose commonly make him a present of a hatchet with a silver handle. (!)

VIII.

The following are Johnson's letters to the King and Queen:

"To the King's most excellent Majesty.

"Sir,—It is most humbly represented to your Majesty by William Dodd, the unhappy convict now lying under sentence of death:

"That William Dodd, acknowledging the justice of the sentence denounced against him, has no hope or refuge but in your Majesty's clemency.

"That though to recollect or mention the usefulness of his life, or the efficacy of his ministry, must overwhelm him, in his present condition, with shame and sorrow; he yet humbly hopes, that his past labours will not wholly be forgotten; and that the zeal with which he has exhorted others to a good life, though it does not extenuate his crime, may mitigate his punishment.

"That debased as he is by ignominy, and distressed as he is by poverty, scorned by the world, and detested by himself, deprived of all external comforts, and afflicted by consciousness of guilt, he can derive no hopes of longer life, but that of repairing the injury he has done to mankind, by exhibiting an example of shame and submission, and of expiating his sins by prayer and penitence.

" That for this end, he humbly implores from the clemency of your Majesty, the continuance of a life legally forfeited; and of the days which, by your gracious compassion, he may yet live, no one shall pass without a prayer, that your Majesty, after a long life of happiness and honour, may stand, at the day of final judgment, among the merciful that obtain mercy.

" So fervently prays the most distressed and wretched of your Majesty's subjects,

" WILLIAM DODD."

" To the Queen's most excellent Majesty.

" MADAM,—It is most humbly represented by Mary Dodd, wife of Doctor William Dodd, now lying in prison under sentence of death :

" That she has been the wife of this unhappy man more than twenty-seven years, and has lived with him in the greatest happiness of conjugal union, and the highest state of conjugal confidence.

" That she has been a constant witness of his unwearied endeavours for public good, and his laborious attendance on charitable institutions. Many are the families whom his care has delivered from want; many are the hearts which he has freed from pain, and the faces which he has cleared from sorrow.

" That, therefore, she most humbly throws herself at the feet of the queen, earnestly entreating, that the petition of a distressed wife asking mercy for a husband, may be considered as naturally soliciting the compassion of her Majesty; and that, when her wisdom has compared the offender's good actions with his crime, she will be pleased to represent his case to our most gracious sovereign, in such terms as may dispose him to mitigate the rigour of the law.

" So prays your Majesty's most dutiful subject and supplicant,

" MARY DODD."

IX.

DOCTOR DODD'S CHARITIES.

(From the *London Chronicle*.)

Magdalen House, Dec. 17, 1767.

It having been already maturely considered, and resolved, that in order to give a stability to this charity, it would be necessary to build a proper house, the present dwelling being no longer in a condition capable of repair for such a purpose, but at an expense which will render a new building far preferable.

At a General Court of the Governors of this Charity held this day, it was resolved:

1. To build a new Magdalen House upon the spot where the present house stands.

2. That the expense of such building shall not exceed 4000*l*.

3. To begin such building as soon as the said sum of 4000*l*. shall be subscribed.

And it was also judged, that as soon as the above resolutions were made known, the friends to this charity would contribute towards so pious an undertaking, every day's experience furnishing the strongest evidence of its real usefulness and humanity.

The following sums have been already subscribed for this purpose; and whatever further assistance may be yet given (to complete the sum), be it little or great, will be very acceptable, and gratefully acknowledged.

A List of Subscribers for building a new Magdalen House :

	£	s.	d.
Her MAJESTY	300	0	0
The Right Hon. the Earl of Hertford, President	100	0	0
Sir George Savile, Bart., one of the Vice-Presidents	100	0	0
Sir Alexander Grant, Bart., one of the Vice-Presidents	100	0	0
Isaac Akerman, Esq.	50	0	0
Thomas Farrar, Esq.	100	0	0
John Anthony Rucker, Esq.	100	0	0
Jonas Hanway, Esq.	20	0	0
Thomas Fletcher, Esq.	52	10	0
Andrew Thompson, Esq.	30	0	0
John Barker, Esq.	100	0	0
Mrs. Barker, by ditto	60	0	0
Mr. John Barker Church, by ditto	40	0	0
John Dorrien, Esq.	50	0	0
The Rev. William Dodd, LL.D.	21	0	0
Philip Milloway, Esq.	30	0	0
John Cornwall, Esq.	30	0	0
George Peters, Esq.	20	0	0
Francis Lawson, Esq.	21	0	0
Mr. Timothy Lacy	21	0	0
Mr. Edward de Sante	21	0	0
George Adey, Esq.	21	0	0
Richard Mothall, Esq.	50	0	0
Messrs. Johnson and Langley	21	0	0
Mr. Sanders Oliver	21	0	0
Joseph Skinner, Esq.	21	0	0
Mr. Samuel Butler	20	0	0

	£	s.	d.
Michael James, Esq.	20	0	0
Mr. Charles Wray	21	0	0
Timothy Mangles, Esq.	21	0	0
Alexander Fordyce, Esq.	52	10	0
George Bristow, Esq.	21	0	0
Peter Duval, Esq.	31	10	0
Albert Nesbitt, Esq.	21	0	0
William Jacomb, Esq.	21	0	0
Peter Bennet, Esq.	31	10	0
Robert Halcrow, Esq.	30	0	0
Edmund Bochm, Esq.	30	0	0
Andrew Grote, Esq., by Mr. de Sante	21	0	0
Jonathan Barnard, Esq.	21	0	0
Mr. Richard Salmon	30	0	0
J. R. Siebel, Esq.	20	0	0
Roger Staples, Esq.	31	10	0
Mr. Isaac Walker	10	10	0
Mr. James Morgan	21	0	0
Mr. Herman Meyer	21	0	0
Mr. Henry A. Langkoff	30	0	0
Mr. Alexander Mahlstede	21	0	0
Vansittart Hudson, Esq.	40	0	0
Mr. William Scholey	21	0	0
Henry Vansittart, Esq.	30	0	0
William Fauquier, Esq.	21	0	0
Robert Baldy, Esq.	21	0	0
Nathaniel Castleton, Esq.	31	10	0
Peter Gaussen, Esq.	21	0	0
Master Philip Stanhope, by Dr. Dodd	21	0	0
Thomas Godfrey, Esq., by Mr. Barker	21	0	0
John Delme, Esq.	50	0	0
Joseph Chaplin Hankey, Esq., by Mr. Skinner	21	0	0
Sundry Persons by the hands of Mr. de Sante	56	14	6
Kirkes Townley, Esq., by Dr. Dodd	21	0	0
James Conningham, Esq.	20	0	0
Stephen Peter Godin, Esq., by Mr. Mangles	50	0	0
John Dick, Esq., by ditto	20	0	0
The Right Hon. Sir Edward Hawke	42	0	0
Robert Nettleton, Esq.	30	0	0

	£	s.	d.
Samuel Rickards, Esq.	25	0	0
Thomas Edward Freeman, Esq.	50	0	0
Samuel Watson, junior, Esq.	21	0	0
Lady Frances Conningsby	100	0	0
William Davidson, Esq.	25	0	0
W. S.	20	0	0
The Right Hon. Lord Orwell	20	0	0
T. H.	1	1	0
Thomas Hanway, Esq.	5	5	0
Mr. Abraham Winterbottom	5	5	0
John Grant, Esq.	10	10	0
Monkhouse Davidson, Esq.	10	10	0
A Gentleman unknown, by Mr. Winterbottom	20	0	0
His Grace the Archbishop of Canterbury	10	10	0
Freeman Flower, Esq.	20	0	0
Paul Blagrave, Esq.	10	10	0
Elisha Biscoe, Esq.	10	0	0
Unknown, by Mr. Hanway	100	0	0
Sir George Pocock	20	0	0
Hon. Baron Perrott	31	10	0
Charles Hornby, Esq.	25	0	0
H. E., by Mr. Milloway	5	5	0
M. Morten Rockcliffe	5	5	0
Capt. Wyville	2	2	0
Dr. Herberden	5	5	0
Hon. Thomas Harvey	20	0	0
Samuel Roffey, Esq.	52	10	0
Mrs. Ann Cottesworth	20	0	0
Laurence Sulivan, Esq.	31	10	0
George Prescot, Esq.	21	0	0

Subscriptions are received by the treasurer, Robert Dingley, Esq., and by the following bankers :—Sir Charles Asgill, Nightingale and Wickenden, Messrs. Brassey, Lee and Son, Messrs. Brown and Collison, Messrs. Martins, Stone and Blackwell, Messrs. Roffey, Neal, James and Fordyce, Messrs. Boldero, Kendal and Adey, in Lombard-street; Messrs. Fuller and Co., Birchin-lane; Sir Joseph Hankey and Partners, Fen-church-street; Messrs. Colebrooke and Co., Thread-needle-street; Messrs. H. R. and R. Hoare, Sir F. Gosling, Gosling and Clive, Messrs. Child and Co., Fleet-street; Messrs. Andrew Drummond and Co., Charing-Cross; Messrs. Backwell and Croft, in Pall-Mall; and the secretary, Mr. Winterbottom, in Threadneedle-street.

The reader will observe the name of "Master Philip Stanhope," by Doctor Dodd, for the large sub-scription of twenty guineas; also that of Lord Orwell, and of Mr. Akerman.

Society for the Discharge and Relief of Persons im-prisoned for Small Debts:

Craven-street, Strand, July 20, 1774.

	£	s.	d.
Benefactions as by the last report . .	5286	5	7
Benefactions received since, viz.:			
S. W.	2	2	0
C. B., second benefaction . . .	1	11	6
C. D., value of two light moidores . . .	2	7	6
	5292	6	7
Since the last advertisement the Society have re-leased 67 prisoners, amounting in all to 2059 (most of whom are useful manufacturers with large families), for the sum of . .	5286	7	7
Balance in hand	5	19	0

From the above state of accounts, the public will

see how small is the balance left in the treasurer's hands, exclusive of the annual benefactions, which have been very lately advertised. Depending, however, on the aid of the generous public, and finding from a variety of applications, and frequent careful inquiries on the subject, that many distressed prisoners, though entitled to relief by the present Insolvent Act, are incapable of paying the fees and expenses necessary on that occasion; the Society have ordered near two hundred persons to be discharged, in the regular course of business, and as expeditiously as possible. Many other prisoners whose circumstances do not come within the intention of the Act, and who are in great distress, wait for relief, and will be discharged so soon as the charity's finances will allow.

Benefactions continue to be received at No. 7, Craven-street, Strand; also at the Thatched House Tavern, in St. James's-street; by Mr. Leacroft, bookseller at Charing-Cross; and at the following bankers, viz.: Messrs. Dorrien, Rucker and Carleton, in Finch-lane, Cornhill; Messrs. Hoares, in Fleet-street; Messrs. Biddulph and Cocks, at Charing-Cross; the London Exchange Banking Company, in St. James's-street; Messrs. Fullers, and Messrs. Lowry and Co., in Lombard-street.

———

Doctor Dodd's programme for reforming young females may be also given here; but its tone leaves a very disagreeable impression, and is quite in the key of his novel, "The Sisters."

To the Author of the London Chronicle.

Sir,—As you have inserted Mr. Fielding's and Mr. Dingley's plans in your paper, and as I have the pleasure to assure you that the beneficent design therein proposed succeeds very happily, I have transmitted to you a pathetic paper, written upon this occasion, and for these plans, by the Reverend Mr. Dodd; which, if you think proper, to insert in your paper, it may serve still more and more to promote the laudable undertaking, to which every member of the community must wish success, and be glad to contribute all the aid in his power.

I am, Sir, your constant reader,

T. G.

London, April 19, 1758.

INTRODUCTION TO A PLAN FOR PRESERVING AND REFORMING YOUNG FEMALES, ETC.

To smoothe the rugged brow of affliction, to soften the severe strokes of calamity, to alleviate the sorrows, and provide kindly remedies for the miseries of our fellow-creatures, must be acknowledged undertakings highly worthy of man, becoming his nature, befitting his place, honourable to himself, and acceptable to his God.

It is pleasing to observe in our nation, famed for its humanity, and justly esteemed for its generosity and benevolence, so many great and public works dedicated to this good end; and in our metropolis especially, so many noble buildings, rising with their awful battlements to heaven, and bearing on their speaking fronts, "sacred to God, to man, to charity, to humanity."

Here the naked are clothed, the hungry fed, the sick, the wounded, the maimed are visited and relieved, helpless innocents rescued from death and from distress; as helpless mothers in the sad moments of their anguish comforted and supported, wretched widows made to sing for joy, deserted orphans sheltered and protected, ignorance instructed, and the strong basis for present and future happiness laid in young and waxen minds. And it deserves serious notice and much congratulation, that though these beneficent undertakings have much increased, during late years, yet the one is not found materially prejudicial to the other; the blessing of God is evidently upon all; for they all flourish, and answer the gracious ends for which they were designed; and no instance can be given of any works of this nature, sinking for want of support, or languishing through deficiency of proper encouragement; an abundant proof of the favourable eye of providence upon them.

Yet though every kind of sufferer seems thus provided with a kindly relief, one species there is which the watchful eye of public benevolence hath hitherto overlooked, whose circumstances nevertheless demand all our compassion, and have a just claim to the tenderest regard. These are those unhappy women, whom one false and fatal step hath plunged in all the miseries of prostitution, and left them no return from shame, from sorrow, from diseases, and from death!

Deluded, perhaps, in the very flower of their youth,

nay, or ere the promising bud is full blown in all its beauty; deceived by flattering vows and impious oaths, betrayed by yielding nature and soft passion, to which all the arts of love, and elegancies of dress and person have laboured to win them; and to which, perhaps, worse arts and viler means have been employed to warm and irritate them: they fall a sacrifice to unbridled lust; which, once satiated, leaves the miserable object a prey to infamy, remorse, and, what is worse, to inevitable destruction!

For who shall receive the ruined outcast? Or what asylum can she find to hide her wretched head? "The world is not her friend, nor the world's law." Shame and pride, the two strongest passions of the mind, prevent a return to those friends, where she is very doubtful either of pardon or reception: lost character forbids admittance under any roof; for who, of the austere and rigid virtuous, will receive or countenance a shameless prostitute? Want and hunger pinch hard; opportunity, too commodious, alas! presents itself; again she plunges into the same dire mischiefs, becomes a slave to lust, and the worse than savage tyranny of bawds and panders. Her wretched situation compels her to the use of intoxicating liquors, that she may destroy all reflection, and be enabled wholly to forget herself; her body, late so fair and beautiful, becomes offensive through loathsome diseases: cast out from every dwelling, she languishes in extreme distress, and foul corruption making every limb its prey; her mind meanwhile no less corrupted, she dies in all the bitterness of anguish here, to enter only on a scene of bitter anguish hereafter!

But, how faint this sketch, how imperfect this draught to set forth the miseries of the numberless unhappy sufferers of this sort who crowd our streets, and nightly are sent out, poor vagabonds, to entice and betray the unwary and unwise, that seek for pleasure where it is never to be found—

> ——Not in the bought smiles
> Of harlots loveless, joyless, unindear'd ;
> Casual fruition.—MILTON.

—and that hope for joy from these, who know no joy, yielding to the lust of others, merely for a horrid maintenance, and to whom, for a few vile pence, every man is equally acceptable !

And yet each one of these have had tender parents, affectionate friends ; each of these have been objects of those parents' cares and wishes, their fond eyes have viewed with delight their infant beauties ; their fond hearts have planned imaginary pleasures, and noted with transport their innocent and promising endearments. Can, then, any parent's eye look otherwise than with feeling compassion on these unhappy objects ; so young, so wretched ? Can any parent's heart do other than bleed and sympathise with the afflicted parents of such ruined daughters ? Can any parent refuse his utmost endeavours, to prevent, as far as may be, so dreadful evils, to restore and retrieve such daughters ; to preserve other daughters from such ruin, other parents from such affliction !

But not as parents only, as fellow-creatures, we see enough in their piteous case to call forth all our compassion, and to cause the exertion of our utmost efforts on their behalf. To see their beauties, from whence their social life derives so much of its comfort, prostituted to the vilest purposes, and abused by the foulest lust; to see them, languishing, decaying, dying, before these beauties are in their bloom: to see those beauties wholly wiped out and defaced by nauseating diseases; and they of late so fair, now so filthy and disgusting, that their once most jovial lovers behold them with horror. What mind on the reflection, but must be filled with gloomy sadness, and a generous distress, but must lament their fate, but would rejoice to have preserved, or to rescue them from it?

But when from the beauties of the body we consider the sad havoc made at the same time with the noble rational mind, when we consider their souls, as men, much more when we consider them as Christians, compassion, humanity, and duty, all call upon us on their behalf. The soft and pleasing tenderness of the sex, their amiable converse, their chaste and modest cheerfulness, serve, above all things, to make life's uneven path smooth and easy, to lighten the burden of care, and soften the frowns of anxiety. But to hear from their lips hoarse and direful curses, torrents of unclean and shameful lasciviousness, sad proofs of their minds' total overthrow; how doth it at once disgust and pain; what a mournful evidence is it of their abandoned profligacy; and how should it quicken us, if possible, to remove that disease also, lest the soul, totally absorbed, perish with the body, and both be lost, eternally lost and undone!

Moved by considerations of this sort, and by a

tender regard to the welfare of their fellow-creatures, it is resolved, by some gentlemen, to attempt a cure for these evils, and to provide an asylum for these sufferers, truly deserving every man's compassion: that when influenced by whatever motive, whether from the body or mind, they are desirous to redeem themselves from their unhappy crimes and situation, they may have a place to fly to, a safe shelter to receive them from the storm. And it is not doubted but every member of the society (to whom these poor objects became a fatal nuisance, by being thus let out nightly in swarms to ruin and decoy) will unite their utmost endeavours to promote the charitable undertaking. The concurrence of all parents is naturally expected: when they view their own daughters, let them learn to pity these, and to yearn on their behalf. And for the gay and gallant, there can be no reason to suppose they will be backward to promote so benevolent a design; whereby they will be empowered to make some little restitution, and to pay a debt of honour and of duty, for the injuries, they may have brought on some of these unhappy objects.* And all Christians, in general, viewing the example of their great lord and master, who came to seek and to save that which was lost, will readily, we are persuaded, join heart and hand, and rejoice to be instrumental in a work, calculated, by God's blessing, to bring many sinners to repentance.

* May I be permitted to hint, over and above the motives Mr. Dodd suggests, an additional one to these gentlemen, which is, "the advantage they have over the women in respect of this crime."

To prevent the destruction of as many as possible, to preserve them from the dire consequences of prostitution above described, and to render them useful, instead of noxious members of the community; must be confessed by far the most eligible method of reforming; this is laying the axe to the root: to preserve the body in health and soundness, is doubtless preferable to the application of severe medicines, or the amputation of corrupted members. And as from the wretched families of the lower class of people in and about this city, uninstructed and profligate sons grow up a nuisance to the community, and commence thieves and robbers; so the daughters, no less ignorant and uninstructed, and exposed to innumerable evils, overrun the streets, desperately abandoned, and even at an age, very frequently, when their minds are scarce capable of consideration.

To preserve the boys a late laudable plan hath been proposed, and happily executed. To preserve the girls, and render them no less useful in their station, to keep them from early prostitution, and early death, and thus to do them and the community signal service —it is proposed, that a house be provided, consisting of two parts, calculated at once for preservation and reformation: the first, the preservatory, for the preservation of such young girls as shall be determined on, and whose circumstances in life would probably lead them to prostitution: the second, the reformatory, for the reception of such, as have been prostituted, and are desirous to repent and reform, &c. See the Plans, *London Chronicle*, p. 149, and p. 348.

This suspicious document suggests the story that went round the papers after his death, of his having once established a house at Bromley, in Kent, for "female boarders, ladies of small fortunes, who were desirous of being introduced into polite life . . . that a coach was kept in the family, and every elegant accommodation that could be required." The scheme answered tolerably well at first, but, adds the account, "the sequel of this narrative we wish could be more favourable in the Doctor's behalf." Some sort of *esclandre* took place, and the establishment was broken up.

X.

Histories of the Tête-à-Tête annexed; or, Memoirs of Sir Simony Scruple and the Subtle Sinner. (From one of the Monthly Magazines, No. 37, 38.)

The period is again arrived, when, agreeable to our promise, we must use our utmost endeavours to re-claim four-and-twenty very polite people, whom we have introduced to our readers in the course of this year as Tête-à-Têtes. We should not be under any apprehensions of not accomplishing our design, had we only to do with the ladies, when we have such a source of persuasive rhetoric at hand, never yet known to fail the learned, agreeable, insinuating* Sir Simony Scruple;

---

* He that has taken his degree at the university is, in the academical style, called Dominus, and in common language was heretofore termed

but as their intimate friends of the other sex may point
out to them the danger of listening to so dangerous a
rival, we must also use our good offices in promoting
his advice and doctrines, which we will, with the
utmost impartiality, set forth, and which must neces-
sarily remove every possible prejudice that can be
raised against him. On his part, we have not the
least doubt (though very scrupulous when the least
infringement is made upon the ecclesiastical rights),
as we do not intend any one pair shall be legally
united, without paying the just fees, agreeable to their
station, that Sir Simony will refuse his clerical
assistance to join in wedlock a dozen couple who
have strayed out of the pale of matrimony ; and in this
persuasion we think ourselves peculiarly happy in
having an opportunity of recommending a gentleman
of Mr. Scruple's elegant appearance and address,
upon so laudable an occasion.

It may appear somewhat singular to many of our
readers, that this gentleman, after having completed
his education at the university, should give the pre-
ference to the pursuits of the law, rather than the
vocation of the gospel ; but it should be remembered
that he was at this time a young man, unexperienced
in the world, hurried away by turbulent passions, and
bewildered by the modish pastimes and polite amuse-

Sir. This was not always a word of contempt ; the graduates assumed
it in their own writings ; so Trevisa the historian writes himself Syr
John Trevisa.—JOHNSON. With how much more propriety may this
be applied to our hero, who has *judiciously* quitted the profane study of
the law, for the pure dictates of the gospel !

ments which surround this great capital; in a word, he had not had at this time any other call than that of nature, to prompt him to action ; and without properly reflecting upon the sin and danger of a life of gaiety and dissipation, he gave in to the fashionable errors so common in youth, and indeed so little exploded by age.

He took chambers in the Temple, and began to study Coke upon Littleton, with as much attention as is generally bestowed by the students of George's and Nando's. He usually breakfasted at the coffee-house, dined at the tavern, took a slice of the play in the pit, supped in a convivial manner in the garden, and the next morning left the dry discussions of John Nokes and Thomas Styles to barristers of fifty, and serjeants past their grand climacteric. A Templer of taste and genius considers the study of the law as only a decent apology for having chambers in the Temple, so instrumental in conducting an intrigue with delicacy, and cornuting an alderman, without prejudicing his lady's reputation. This is a science pursued with infinite more labour and industry in this seminary of jurisprudence, than in any spot of the same extent under the sun. The seraglios of the East may be filled with confined sultanas; but in this land of liberty free egress and regress is allowed every female devoted to Venus, who pays her devotion in this Temple, so immediately consecrated to that goddess, and where the numbers are at least equal to those of the Grand Signior's harem.

Mr. Scruple, whose conscience at this time was not

contracted by any of those puritanic notions he has since imbibed, was soon initiated into all the mysteries of the Temple. Being then a genteel, agreeable young fellow, master of an uncommon share of address, possesssed of that degree of assurance so necessary to carry a man through life upon every critical occasion, and being also naturally of an amorous disposition (though like Socrates, we must now suppose he has completely suppressed it by philosophy or methodism), he failed not to avail himself of those talents so bountifully bestowed upon him by our common parent. To aver the truth, few fellow-students had more intrigues upon their hands than young Scruple: Simony had almost a constant levee and succession of beauties, from the Honourable Mrs. D—— down to Betty L——, his sempstress; and he timed his appointments so well, and was so happily calculated for prosecuting his business, that no one of his numerous mistresses ever suspected she had a rival.

In this round of pleasure and dissipation our hero moved for near five years, without any alloy, or one single pang of conscience intruding upon the felicity of his hours. His vanity was, indeed, gratified on every side; for whilst the ladies admired him for the elegance and symmetry of his person, the wits and critics paid the highest encomiums on his taste and judgment: he was courted by living authors for his profound knowledge of the dead; and the dramatic writers curried his favour, that the Bedford and George's might not receive the first lash of literary d——n to their works from the breath of Scruple.

When the time approached of his being called to the bar, he began to find that he had made very little progress in the law; and that in all probability he would, from his ignorance in the science, not only make a very contemptible figure in the court of King's Bench, but that more likely his practice would not defray the expense of coach-hire, even in the usual *party quarré* during term time. His patrimony, which was originally not considerable, he had greatly diminished, and the residue of it would scarcely support him a twelvemonth in his usual gaiety and expense. These considerations brought him to some serious reflections, and these ruminations carried him one evening to St. Dunstan's, where he heard the great Romaine. He caught the enthusiastic fire of devotion—was from that moment a proselyte, and resolved soon to be a preacher.

Let it not astonish our readers to find, that talents which would starve a man in Westminster Hall, may make his fortune in a pulpit: the genius that forms an excellent pathetic preacher, may make but a very contemptible pleader; and yet in Scruple how easy the transition, from the glorious uncertainties of the law, to the ideal jargons of methodism!

We may now suppose that Mr. Simony Scruple has quitted his chambers in the Temple, his gallantry, intrigues, convivial companions, playhouse critics, and coffee-house politicians, and like a man new made, having a proper call, is regenerated into a pious divine.

The reverend Sir Simony soon made himself conspicuous as a preacher: he had many followers, even

in the circles of Grosvenor and Berkeley squares, and
in a short time he had the care of the souls of many
women of quality, whose former irregularities began
to prey upon their consciences, and make them think
it was time for them to have a spiritual guide. On
his part he did everything to comfort them and as-
suage their affliction, as he did not, like his brethren
W——d, W——y, and R——ne, preach up near so
much damn——n; and offered them hopes of happiness in this world, as well as that to come. The
orthodoxy of his doctrine prevailed beyond his most
sanguine expectations, and he was esteemed the
politest methodist preacher that ever banged a pulpit.
In proportion as his fame extended his purse increased,
and he found profit and honour flow in on every side.

It was at the time he had attained this zenith of
renown that the affair from which he has so justly
derived his title, occurred, and made him still more
talked of, than his preaching or his doctrines. Mr.
K., the patron of the living of Al——kle, being embarrassed in his circumstances, at the time the living
was vacant in 1763, he proposed disposing of the
perpetual advowson. A purchaser had agreed for it
at the price of eleven hundred pounds, but within
fourteen days of a lapse, repented of his bargain, and
threw up the agreement. In this dilemma the unfortunate patron applied to Mr. Scruple for his
advice, and it was agreed that the living should be
put into the hands of some person who should hold it
for a limited time. Mr. Scruple recommended Mr.
II.,* his deputy and dependent, and this pious gen-

* It is with unfeigned pleasure we can acquaint our readers that

tleman " was" (to use his own words) " ready to stand
in the gap." Mr. K., confiding in their integrity,
gave Mr. H. the living in the year 1764: from that
time Mr. K. frequently applied to the two reverend
gentlemen, earnestly requesting them to consider and
compassionate his case, either to make him satisfaction, by purchasing the advowson, or consent to a
resignation, as the disappointment he had met with in
this transaction had been the ruin of him and his
family. But so religiously bent upon justice were
these charitable gentlemen, that though thoroughly
convinced of the patron's distress, they refused to
make him any sort of recompense, because it would
be—Simonical! By this legal refusal of restoring the
living, or making any kind of acknowledgment for
it, they piously possess one hundred and thirty-five
pounds per annum, for which they paid nothing—but
a little wholesome advice in favour of themselves.

It was upon this occasion that Mr. Foote introduced in his comedy of " The Devil upon Two
Sticks" that justly satirical stroke, where he says,
" Simony is a new devised canon of our modern
saints, which makes it not criminal to betray one's
trust, and piously plunder the little property of an
indigent man and his family." When a man has
once got a good name, he may do anything with impunity: we have plenty of proverbs in support of

this worthy limb of Methodism is this month fortunately united in
wedlock to a lady, possessed not only (in the style of our news-writers)
of every accomplishment necessary to render the marriage state happy,
but to recompense the many uncommon social virtues of her pious
husband.

this opinion; but the followers of Scruple are still greater evidences of the rectitude of the assertion. His fame was no way diminished by this public act of injustice, his chapel was as crowded, his pews were filled with as good company, and his female disciples were as anxious as ever for his pious labours in their behalf. Husbands, so far from entertaining the least shadow of jealousy at his frequent visits to their wives in their absence, ascribed to his valuable exhortations many virtues they had never before discovered in their ladies. Among the foremost of these was a reformation in point of gaming and vigils, which hurt their constitutions, and in many had hitherto so greatly impaired them, that they had been prevented being mothers, and giving heirs to great titles and large estates; an evil that had been in a great measure removed by the excellent precepts of the reverend reformer.

Sir Simony's renown in this respect reached the ears of the comely Subtle Sinner, who had been married to her worthy mate near twenty years, and yet their wealth was likely to devolve to a second cousin. This lady's husband was just returned from the East Indies, with an Asiatic fortune and a broken constitution. She resolved upon being a disciple to the justly-admired orator, and accordingly purchased a seat in his chapel, which she constantly attends every time he preaches.

Our heroine took the earliest opportunity of giving Sir Simony a general invitation to her house, and he was too polite to refuse a lady's mandate. The nabob was not, however, of so tractable a turn as many of the helpmates of Sir Simony's female disciples. He had his scruples as well as the divine, but they were of a different complexion. In vain he remonstrated with his good lady to dismiss their clerical guest : the more urgent he was against Sir Scruple's visits, the more firmly resolved she was to admit of them. His doubts, his suspicions, his jealousy, were hence increased. He communicated his apprehensions to a trusty valet, with whom it was concerted to watch all Simony's motions. A letter was intercepted from the Subtle Sinner to the preacher, penned in such terms as redoubled every alarm ; and the Asiatic plumb resolved to inflict the punishment of an Abelard on Scruple if the event corroborated his guilt. Luckily for the pious teacher, the nabob was seized with a fit of the gout that very afternoon, which confined him to his room ; and the valet was troubled with some pious qualms, that made him refuse executing the commission.

These pious qualms of the valet were in some degree owing to the perusal of one of his mistress's good books, which operated so strongly upon him that he was convinced Sir Simony was a worthy pastor, who had been grossly injured by a supposititious letter ; and resolving instantly to become one of his flock, he may now be seen in the front of the gallery, sighing and sobbing with the old ladies every time Scruple preaches. The blabbing valet had, however, a few nights before his conversion, thrown out some hints in the company of an Irish gentleman (who had repaired to this metropolis to make his fortune, either by the aid of the blind goddess at the hazard-table, or some equally blind mortal female, at the still more hazardous game of matrimony) that the Subtle Sinner was certainly very fond of Sir Simony, and, after drinking a few more glasses, mentioned the precise place of their rendezvous, at the same time giving a description of the Methodist's person and dress. The Hibernian hero, not ignorant of the advantages that might be derived from such an alliance, resolved to personate his reverend rival. He accordingly hired a gown and cassock, with a proper peruke, and repairing to the place of assignation, had already given the lady a lecture upon moral philosophy before her expected master arrived. When Sir Simony came he was denied admittance, and, like Castalio, in " The Orphan," cursed the unfaithful sex for the deception. The next day (after he had sermonised near Hyde Park-corner) an *éclaircissement* took place. She vowed she thought she perceived a difference ; and that, to own the truth, she now found she must have been imposed upon, for that she greatly preferred the usual teaching of Sir Simony.

It is above four months since the Subtle Sinner has been a convert to his doctrines, and the benefit she has already reaped from them is incredible. She has not once touched a card, or sat up after twelve during this period, and as her husband is now gone to Bath for the recovery of his health, there are great hopes, from Sir Scruple's constant visits and efficacious exhortations, that, in a short time, the great object of all her pious wishes will be accomplished, as she seems still every way capable of doing justice to posterity, and making amends for the time lost by her husband's absence. Our engraver has communicated a very striking likeness of her person, which must convince the observer that she is of that complexion to profit by the orthodox labours of her worthy pastor.

XI.

The following advertisement is quite characteristic of the Doctor's "sensational" administration of the Magdalen charity. The delivery of the "two tickets for the church" with "each ticket for the feast" is admirable.

MAGDALEN HOSPITAL.

THE Anniversary Meeting of the Governors of this Hospital, will be held at DRAPERS' HALL, in Throgmorton-street, on Thursday, the 25th day of this instant April, after a Sermon to be preached at the parish church of St. George's, Hanover-square, before the Right Hon. the Earl of HERTFORD, President, the Vice-Presidents, Treasurer, and the rest of the Governors, by the Rev. John Craven, A.M., Rector of Woolverton, in the county of Southampton, and chaplain to the Right Hon. the Earl of Denbigh.

Prayers will begin at Eleven o'clock.
Dinner on table at half-past Three precisely.

STEWARDS.

Sir Robert Clayton, Bart.	John Regnier, Esq.
Sir George Pocock, Knight of the Bath.	Robert Salmon, Esq.
	Philip Stanhope, Esq.
John Shakespeare, Esq., and Alderman.	James Vere, Esq.
	John Weyland, Esq.
The Hon. Thomas Harvey.	Robert Wilsonn, Esq.

Te Deum, Jubilate, and several new Anthems adapted to the charity, will be performed in the course of the service.

Two tickets for the church will be delivered with each ticket for the feast.

Tickets for the church or feast will be delivered to the order in writing of any governor by the secretary, Mr. Winterbottom, at No. 32, Threadneedle-street, London.

Dinner tickets at 5s. each with two tickets for the church may be had at the following places:—Waghorne's Coffee-house, in the Court of Requests; Arthur's, St. James's-street; Mount Coffee-house, Grosvenor-street; Richard's Coffee-house, near Temple-bar; Batson's, John's and Tom's, Cornhill.

Even the ordinary advertisements of his books have the old "Dodd-like" flavour:

West Ham, February 24, 1764.

MR. DODD begs leave to inform his Friends and the Public, that his COMMENTARY on the SACRED SCRIPTURES, with Mr. LOCKE'S ANNOTATIONS, has been for some time in the press; but he has determined to postpone the publication till October next, that the sheets may be sufficiently dry and fit for use. In the mean time a specimen of the work may be seen at Mr. Davis's, the corner of Sackville-street, Piccadilly; Mr. Newbery's, in St. Paul's Church-yard; and at Messrs. Davis and Reymer's, in Holborn. And if any friends to Sacred Literature shall please to communicate their observations on any parts of the Scriptures, due respect will be paid to them in the course of the work; as no pains or attention are spared to render the Commentary complete and useful, and such as may answer the wishes of those who desire to see a free and rational interpretation of the Scriptures.

ADVERTISEMENT.

DR. DODD'S COMMENTARY on the BIBLE, which began to be published in April, 1765, being now far enough advanced to enable him to ascertain the number of sheets it will contain; he thinks proper to inform the subscribers and the public, that it will be comprised within 190 numbers; and that a republication is going to be made from the beginning. The materials are great, but due care has been and will be taken not unnecessarily to swell the work. Those who are inclined to encourage this undertaking, but postponed giving their orders till they could know the quantity it would make, have now an opportunity of beginning with No. I. and being served progressively, either in weekly or monthly numbers.

On Saturday, May 10, will be republished,

NUMBER I. of

THE HOLY BIBLE.

Printed on a large and beautiful type, and illustrated with a Commentary and practical improvements. In these are inserted the Notes and Collections of John Locke, Esq., the Rev. Daniel Waterland, D.D., the Right Hon. Edward Earl of Clarendon, and other learned persons.

By WILLIAM DODD, LL.D.,

Prebendary of Brecon, and Chaplain in Ordinary to his Majesty.

N.B. This work will be regularly republished, in both weekly and monthly numbers; the first will contain three large sheets, inclosed in blue paper, and be delivered every Saturday, price 6d., and the last will contain twelve sheets, and will be published the first day of every month, and delivered with the magazines, price 2s.

Proposals at large may be had of the proprietors, R. Davis, in Piccadilly; J. Newbery, St. Paul's Church-yard; L. Davis and C. Reymers, Holborn; also of the publisher, F. Newbery, Paternoster-row; and of all booksellers and news-carriers.

The former publication of this work is carried on as usual, and will be continued till the whole is completed.

By the prominent position given to the following notices of the Doctor's motions, it will be seen what a remarkable public character he was considered:

Yesterday the Reverend Doctor Dodd preached before their Majesties, and their Royal Highnesses the Dukes of Gloucester and Cumberland, at the Chapel Royal, St. James's. The sword of state was carried to and from chapel by the Right Hon. Lord Cadogan.

On Monday the Reverend Doctor Dodd had the honour to present to his Royal Highness the Prince of Wales a volume of sermons on the " Duties of the Great," which their Majesties have permitted him to dedicate to the Prince, and which were most graciously received.

Yesterday morning the new chapel in Charlotte-street, near Buckingham-gate, was opened, and a sermon preached to a numerous audience by the Reverend Doctor Dodd. In the afternoon the same gentleman preached his farewell sermon at St. Olave, Hart-street, he having resigned the lectureship of that parish, and for which there are several candidates.

To-morrow the Earl of Hertford, President of the Magdalen House, the Vice-Presidents, Treasurer, &c., are to meet at Charlotte Chapel, near the Queen's Palace, and after divine service, and a sermon by the Reverend Doctor Dodd, will go to St. George's-fields and lay the first foundation-stone of the new intended building for that charity, and afterwards dine at the London Tavern.

In regard to the "Simony" affair, a letter was addressed to the papers giving the Doctor's own version, which betrays the hand of Governor Thicknesse. It does not improve his case:

To the Printer.

SIR,—Had it not been for the unfortunate letter supposed to be wrote by an unfortunate man to a very fortunate one, I am thoroughly satisfied he would have withheld his hand from that deed which brought such severe affliction on himself, his family, and friends; and therefore his own account of that story, which he told me soon after it came out, and confirmed again a short time before he suffered, ought to be publicly known.

Upon my expressing my surprise that he could have been so injudicious in taking so direct a line to preferment, he expressed an equal surprise that I could suppose him so totally ignorant of the world, but added, that two women, one nearly related to him, and another (very rich) warmly attached to his family and interest, had laid their heads together to surprise him with this great piece of preferment, and then observed that the affection he bore for one, and the obligations he lay under to the other, determined him to bear the imputation of folly, rather than expose the weakness of his two best friends. This was his uniform account of the matter to me, when that offence was recent, and since it has been covered by a greater; nor can his enemies advance but one single reason to suppose him capable of taking that weak step, *i.e.* his having taken that for which he suffered since. Thus much I know to be true, that a certain rich lady (since dead) did at times make Mrs. D—— very liberal presents, and there is nothing extraordinary in supposing that such a woman might agree to advance a considerable sum of money, in order to advance a man for whom, and his family, she had a most particular regard. The unfortunate man seemed from the first moment that affair and the consequences became public, to sink, and to be in the state of a poor girl, who, being seduced by a lover, and discarded by her friends, becomes a common prostitute, more from necessity than choice. When once a man has lost his good name, he loses the strongest tie to keep him a good man. I wish he had found mercy where mercy is to be found: were it for no other reason but that I know, great as his crime was, he had suffered punishment enough before he left Newgate, for a crime even of a deeper dye. Greater criminals have been pardoned; greater criminals will be pardoned. He was a great object of justice, but he was also a greater object of mercy. After what he had suffered in confinement, if he was really a believer himself, there cannot be a doubt but that his life would have been a more useful one to society than his death was an example. His address to his fellow-prisoners, and his resignation and composed behaviour, prove him to have been a Christian penitent; and he often assured me, that if his life was spared, the remainder of it should be employed in the practice as well as the preaching of piety. Perhaps, if he had employed his pen on the favourable side in politics, it might have done him more service than in matters of religion. Perhaps, his having latterly employed it another way, did him no service with the Tories.

The voice of the people is the voice of God.

––––––

A RELATION OF THE BEHAVIOUR OF DOCTOR DODD IN NEWGATE, ETC.

Doctor Dodd, though by his own confession he had for some years past indulged himself in a voluptuous life, yet, after his confinement, lived with great temperance, according to Mr. Villette the Ordinary of Newgate's account; though he might, as he himself said, have lived luxuriously, through the benevolence of his friends.

Mr. Villette says, that as several of the stories spread abroad against the Doctor came to his ears, he thought it incumbent on him to ask him several questions relative to the truth of them ; and that he answered in such a manner, as plainly evinced that MOST of them were absolutely false, or greatly and inhumanly exaggerated. It is to be wished that Mr. Villette had expressed himself more fully and explicitly on this subject.

The Doctor employed part of his time in amending a Book of Devotions for the Use of Prisoners, written by one Rossell, as appears by a letter he wrote to the ordinary :

" DEAR SIR,—In consequence of our conversation, I have perused Rossell's book* with attention. There is a great deal of good matter in it, but ill-digested, and often very ill expressed. I have been at much pains to reform what appeared to me erroneous, and to arrange what is irregular and confused. To say the truth, I have spent many hours in an endeavour to render his work more uniform, and consequently more useful. How far I have succeeded, I cannot tell; for I freely own to you, that his multiplicity of chaotic matter has often so entangled and perplexed me, that I have been scarce master of my own ideas, and, I verily believe, could have composed a work on the subject with less trouble than it has cost me to revise this. And, after all, I am doubtful whether the upshot of the matter, in this arrangement, will not be the same with me, as with those who, under a notion of saving expenses, repair, add to, and reform an old building, which, after all, is but an old one, and in the end commonly turns out as expensive, though by no means so commodious, as one entirely new would have proved. Of this, however, you, sir, must be the best judge, whose experience on these heads is preferable to any mere ideas of my poor brain, especially in its present disturbed and unsettled state. Had I been master of more leisure, or longer time, I think I could have made the book better, and more calculated to answer its humane design. As it is, and solicitous as I am to improve every moment in my present awful state, you will accept what I have done as a little tribute of my good will to you, and as a proof that I

* A Book of Devotions for the Use of Prisoners.

am desirous, in every situation, to do all in my humble power to contribute a mite to the best welfare of my fellow-creatures. I could wish that a short Address to my unhappy fellow-prisoners, which I have written, and will communicate to you, might be prefixed to the work; as, perhaps, from the sad singularity of my unfortunate circumstances, it may gain more attention from them than the much better labours of another person. That God may bless and assist you in the performance of your doleful but necessary and important office, is, sir, the fervent prayer of

" Your dying brother,

" (In our common Lord)

" WILLIAM DODD."

He was led by the flattery of his friends, before the order for execution arrived, that he should find mercy. One of his friends had, some days before, sent him a congratulatory letter upon obtaining his pardon, which he told him he heard was procured through the intercession of the Prince of Wales. His mind was, in consequence, greatly agitated between hope and fear, so that he had a very distressed night before the order came, and was not well prepared for the dreadful news. His friends began to open it to him by degrees, but he requested them to tell him the truth at once; for he imagined by their countenances how the matter was. He told the ordinary soon after, that he had only indulged himself for the three preceding days with hopes of mercy from what his friends had said to him; for that he had all along, even from his first entrance into the gaol, given himself up as a lost man. After the first shock of the news of his being included in the death warrant was subsided, he became more composed, and his mind, in general, intent upon a preparation for death.

During his confinement he had a number of letters sent to him from different persons, among which was the following letter from the Right Honourable the Countess of Huntingdon:

" REVEREND SIR,—From the first hearing of your unfortunate situation, I could not look for any less supplies of support and comfort for you, than to Him who chose for our sakes to be numbered with the transgressors. You are master of every rational and scripture argument, and in this, perhaps, inferior to few. And I earnestly pray God these may have their place, and their times of consolation for you.

" But reason, or the wisest conclusions drawn from even truth itself, neither removes the stings of guilt, nor possesses the soul with that peace, which ever passes the best informed understanding. O no! nothing but that voice of Almighty power that spoke from the Cross to your suffering companion there, can be your point now: and we all, like him, must pass sentence upon ourselves, and say, We indeed receive the due reward of our deeds. How soon the welcome request, Lord remember me, &c., reached the heart of our divine substitute; how speedy the relief; how lasting and complete the comfort. The meaning of my prayers and tears for your grief, would have no other language but Go and do thou likewise. Forgive, and do not wonder you should find my views so

limited as this seems for your only relief. Were life
extended to its latest possible period, the alone solid
or well-grounded hope of happiness must subsist
purely by this interior blessing; as making the little
good we have on earth have all its safety, and all the
various evils of a miserable world wisely or rationally
supported by it. Thus everything unites to render
the importunity of your suffering heart the happy
subject of this mercy. This mercy, once obtained,
will bear you through the fluctuating emotions, and
various views of life and death, which so immediately
and naturally operate upon you, and even cause you
to glory in tribulation.

" May you thus rejoice in the truth and power of
that religion you have so long professed and taught
to others, and becoming a witness of our Saviour's
grace to sinners, be enabled to preach the best sermon
you ever preached in your life, and to people the most
miserable and ignorant of the high Christian privilege
of salvation by the cross of our Lord Jesus Christ!
Should He answer the affectionate cries of his poor
unworthy people for you, and that arm of infinite
consolation be stretched out for your strength and
eternal blessedness, how little will the appendages of
death appear, which to mere suffering nature is so
bitter; and how thankfully will you see Justice and
Mercy thus met together, and mixed in that cup, so
severe in the eyes of others; or should the tender
compassions of royal mercy be extended to save from
the present suffering hour, yet only in life, or in the
more remote event of death, this grace must be the
one cause of praise, through time and eternity for

you. It is for this I would most affectionately recommend you day and night. And it is to Him who
is able to do abundantly above all we can ask or
think; and thus I beg to remain a sympathising
friend, and, reverend sir,

"Your humble Servant,

"S. HUNTINGDON.

"S. Wales."

Books of very different contents were also sent to
him; so that he had such a collection of different
systems of doctrine forced upon him in books and
letters, as might, according to the ordinary's expression, distress and perplex any human being. He was
also visited by persons of very different sentiments
and complexions, but always mentioned his satisfaction when visited by men of sense and piety. Among
others, he spoke respectfully of Mr. Wesley, and likewise of Mr. Romaine, who paid him a visit a short
time before his death: from the last of these gentlemen he received peculiar comfort, and said that they
parted mutually satisfied. He frequently appeared to
have a deep sense of his past offences; and expressed,
when he reflected upon the great love of God in the
redemption of the world through Christ, his unworthiness, and a great abhorrence of his ingratitude
towards Him in having deviated from Him and His
divine precepts: this he often did with tears. He
frequently bemoaned his having brought such a dishonour upon religion, and upon the sacred function;
and declared with great emotion, that if he could wipe
off the offence he had thus given, he would gladly

R

submit to the greatest tortures; and would rather die than return into the world again to offend his God, and act inconsistent with His holy will. He often expressed his willingness to die a natural death, but painful apprehensions of a public execution, attended with all the tragic, and yet disorderly parade, usual in this country. He spoke of the execution of others who had suffered on account of their crimes, and said he did not think that heroism was a proper state of mind for such; humble hope was the highest they could aspire to : heroism and triumph belonged to martyrs. He uttered frequently his thankfulness that he had enjoyed so much composure of mind, health, and comfortable rest, free from any distressing dreams, since his confinement, and found himself more happy after his detection than before. He said that he esteemed his affliction as a fatherly correction from God, to bring him into those paths of rectitude from which he had for some years erred.

The day before his execution, he expressed what a trial it would be to take a final leave of his wife, who had been remarkably affectionate to him during the twenty-seven years they had been married. In the evening of the same day, after he was in his room, he said, "Now the bitterness of death is past." He then related that he had taken a tender leave of his friends, and from his dearest friend, his wife. He said, "I was much afraid of this scene, but it passed over much easier than I could have possibly imagined, and Mrs. Dodd behaved on the occasion better than I expected : we parted as those who hope to meet again." He declared repeatedly, and yet with deep contrition, his readiness to die, and that he relied wholly and confidently on the merits of his Lord and Saviour. He spoke of the love of God in Christ Jesus with peculiar energy, and with such a sense of his own unworthiness as was a proof that he was sincere, and that his resignation to the execution of justice was not at all dissembled, but genuine. He praised the Lord for the great work of redemption, by which sinners could be saved; and compared the great difference between the death of the most renowned heathens, who lost all sight of their evil actions, and that of the humble, contrite Christian, who saw at one view the wisdom, holiness, and justice of God, and at the same time His infinite love and mercy in the salvation of sinners by Jesus Christ. He had sometimes expressed his thoughts about our penal laws, that they were too sanguinary; that they were against not only the laws of God, but of nature; and that his own case was hard; that he should die for an act which he always declared to be wrong, but by which he never intended to injure any one individual; and that as the public had forgiven him, he thought he might have been pardoned. But now he laid all these thoughts touching himself aside, though he continued to think in the same manner of the penal laws to his end.

Upon the coming in of a faithful and steady friend, and a clergyman, he said, among other things, " I have requested of my friends to-day what I now request also of you. It is possible that, after my death, some of my kind friends, who have so earnestly solicited my pardon, but in vain, and others, may charge the king and his councillors with cruelty, and use improper language out of love to me; make it known, that I declare this to be far from my thoughts : I love and honour the king; I doubt not his humanity: he and his councillors have acted according to justice; and his Majesty would have extended mercy, if he could have thought it consistent with the welfare of the nation." He then lifted up his hands, and prayed, "O Almighty God, thou King of Kings, bless our gracious king; support and strengthen him, establish his throne in righteousness; give peace in his day, O Lord; make an end of dissension, and put a stop to the present unnatural war. O give his councillors wisdom, and bless them. Amen." After this, going to prayer, he shed many tears, and concluded with saying, "O Lord Jesus Christ, let a poor sinner yet speak unto Thee, though unworthy : O strengthen my faith, comfort and support me, have mercy upon me, and forgive me my sins, for the sake of Thy holy, precious blood. Amen." He said, that if the Lord would leave it to his choice to be now annihilated, by which means all would be over, or that he should die, and stand the chance of eternal life, or eternal misery, he would not give up his hope of the glorious inheritance, no, not for ten thousand worlds.

On the morning of his execution he appeared composed, and being asked how he had been supported, he said he had had some comfortable sleep, whereby he should be the better enabled to perform his duty.

In the curious Dodd miscellany belonging to Mr. Forster, are some characteristic engravings relating to the execution. One is of the Doctor "taken from life in Newgate, the morning of the execution," and represents him in a decent suit of black, and the full-bottomed wig; but in an affected and dramatic attitude. Another is far more characteristic, showing Dodd and Harris on the fatal cart, each attended by his clergyman, with the rows of spectators, constables, sheriffs, hangman, and other actors. It is excellently drawn, and, curiously enough, the artist's name was Dodd. A third illustration is in the rude style peculiar to chap books, and shows the Doctor swinging in the air, with the "eye of Providence" looking down, and Mrs. Dodd weeping at one side.

The whole of Doctor Dodd's career, from his first appearance as a preacher to his "fatal exit at Tyburn," was worked into an effective Surrey melodrama, not many years back. The hero was played with excellent spirit by Mr. Cowper, and the Doctor's tastes for dissipation afforded an opportunity of introducing Ranelagh and other effective scenes of amusement. "Doctor Dodd" had a long run.

REVIVIFICATION AFTER HANGING, p. 180.

" The subjoined incident we had from a friend, whose father was high sheriff of Tyrone about forty years ago. A country lad was hung at Omagh, for sheep-stealing; a penalty and offence frequently associated at that epoch. After the prescribed time

s

the criminal was cut down and delivered to his friends for interment. They made the usual attempt at reviving him, and in this instance succeeded. The man recovered, retaining no outward marks of what had happened beyond a slight distortion of the neck. It was thought by many he had no right to be amongst the living, and that unholy agencies had helped him. He was shunned by his former companions, could obtain no work, and wandered about an alms-beggar. Necessity drove him to the house of the gentleman who, in his official duty, had superintended the execution. He recognised, relieved, and dismissed him, not being disposed to pursue the matter further. But, first, as a physical inquiry, asked him to describe his sensations on being turned off. He replied that he felt the jerk, but not so acutely as to produce insensibility or even confusion. He appeared to have the power of looking above, below, and around. All was of a bright vermilion colour. An agreeable sensation then crept through his frame until he became insensible. " But," he added, " I can find no words to express the agony of gradually returning to consciousness !" Necessity, or natural bent, or what modern cant would call " his mission," drove him back to his old trade, which drove him again to the gallows, but this time without benefit of resuscitation."—*Dublin University Magazine, January,* 1865.

THE END.

LONDON:
PRINTED BY C. WHITING, BEAUFORT HOUSE, STRAND.